ENEMY BOSS'S BABY SURPRISE

CALLIE STEVENS

1

———

KIRA

ONE YEAR EARLIER...

Fuck. Why does this keep happening to me?

"Kira, Kira, Kira!"

I stop in my tracks and whip back around to look at my assistant.

Polly's hand is resting on a door handle. She points at the door with an anxious expression. "In *here*."

I've been walking so fast I just blew right past the door to the conference room. "What would I do without you?" I whisper fondly.

The older blonde woman smiles, her apple cheeks tightening. "Miss out on meetings by working through them, probably."

Polly opens the door for me, and I slither in, trying to go unnoticed as I move to the back of the room.

Trevor Wynters, our CEO, is amid his keynote.

"Thank you all for joining me here today. As you know, Wynters Group has had our best year yet. Through our ingenuity and forward-thinking, we have maintained our spot as the foremost application and program creators of the twenty-first century."

Trevor Wynters is as good as they come. If it weren't for him, I wouldn't have gotten my chance in tech as early as I did. This was my first job out of college.

I'm not even sure I'd still have this job if it weren't for him. But I do, and I appreciate him so much, I do my best job just to keep him happy. He lets me be me, and I work my ass off to be one of his best programmers.

He is the sole reason why I don't foresee anything pulling me away from this place.

"I could take the time to call out each and every one of you for your contributions. Truly, it's hard to fathom that a little mail-order catalog from the early nineteen hundreds has blossomed into what Wynters Group represents today. Unfortunately, we don't have the time for that today. I'm sure the finger food would be cold by the time I was finished and god forbid that."

Trevor's audience lets out a polite chuckle. I do too, giving a sidelong glance to Henry, one of my fellow app developers who already has a plate full of finger food and a bacon-wrapped date shoved in his mouth.

"So, let me cut to the chase, huh? I'm not one for doing that, but I think today calls for it." Trevor clears his throat and lifts his chin high, tossing his long waves of gray hair from his eyes.

"Over the next two years, I will be making my exit as CEO of Wynters Group."

My heart plunges into my stomach.

Polly grabs my arm and squeezes. We lock terrified eyes. Words aren't really necessary right now to know what the other is thinking.

Trevor holds his hands up as if he's prepared for an onslaught of gasps. "I know what you're thinking. In this day and age, upheaval in the corporate sector is a recipe for disaster. But as is the Wynters way, we're keeping things in the family."

From the head table, someone stands. A tall man with dark hair.

He traverses the space up to the stage and stands next to Trevor.

I've seen him in the hallways before. Always looking rather grumpy and standoffish. I thought he was just some disgruntled accountant. Never in a million years would I have guessed he was...

"My son, Orlie, will be taking over as CEO for Wynters Group so that I can retire. Orlie will usher the Wynters Group into a new era. One of intense progress and exciting innovation. I have instilled in my boy my values. He will value your loyalty, your commitment, and, most importantly, your humanity. That's what has put us apart from our competitors since nineteen-oh-one."

I'm not a person that shows her emotions at the best of times. Or at all, except when it comes to my family. Maybe. I can remain cool and passive in most situations even when my feelings are wreaking havoc.

But right now, I can almost feel my face falling as the corners of my lips droop lower and lower.

Orlie Wynters hasn't even cracked a smile.

How are we supposed to believe he's anything like his father if he looks like the corporate robot Trevor has worked so hard not to become?

"A few words, Orlie?"

Orlie clears his throat and leans to the mic. He's taller than his father, meaning he has to stoop down so his voice registers on the microphone. "I look forward to this endeavor and all the prosperity to come."

Polly leans into me. "How many times do you think he practiced that in the mirror?"

I cover my mouth with my hand and try not to laugh. She's right.

He is even worse than I am. That man has never felt an emotion a day in his life.

"So, with that, I encourage you all to get to know Orlie. He'll be around more and more as I pull back gradually. This change will be slow so I ask you all to please be open with your feelings as we try and usher Wynters into a new era," Trevor looks around the room, taking us all in. "Now, I know you've all been waiting for your dismissal. Enjoy the buffet."

While the people at the tables start to rise and flood over to the buffet tables, Polly and I turn to one another, two of only a few women amongst a sea of tech bros.

I am in shock right now. "What is Trevor thinking?"

Polly nods. "That he wants to spend the rest of his days deep-sea fishing, I'm sure."

I sigh. "I mean, he deserves that. He deserves to retire, but..."

"I guess it's better to promote someone from inside the company rather than do some search. Companies always seem to fall apart when they bring in outsiders."

"Yeah, but it's still nepotism."

Polly shrugs. "Fair. That's been the Wynters way since the beginning, though."

"Yeah..."

"You didn't want a chance to be CEO, did you?" she elbows me in the side.

Alarm bells go off in my head. "Me?! No. Never in a million years. I just don't know if Orlie can live up to –"

Trevor Wynter's voice rises above the others. "Kira!"

I stand up stock straight at the sound of Trevor Wynters calling my name. I look in his direction on the outskirts of the room. He waves me over with his signature pleasant smile.

Standing next to him is his son.

"Shit."

Polly gives me a sheepish smile. "It will be great."

"I don't know, that guy looks like his bite is worse than his bark."

"Oh, hush and go talk to him," she bumps my hip.

That little bump propels me across the room to meet Trevor and Orlie. Trevor used to make me nervous the first year I was here. Now, though, I consider him a friend. As much as he can be for being my multi-billionaire boss.

However, the closer I get, the harder my heart beats in my chest.

Trevor slides his hand over my back with a paternal smile. "I wanted you to meet Orlie officially." He looks at his son. "This is the woman I was telling you about. Kira Solace."

I try to smile at Orlie. His lips don't even move. He just nods. "Nice to meet you, Ms. Solace."

I've never seen Orlie up this close. But what I see is making my mouth dry. Anytime he's passed me in the hall, he's kept his gaze down to the ground.

Now, though, I can see his eyes. Darker than dark. Black holes that could suck me in.

Something about that is intriguing.

"I wouldn't say this in front of the rest of them, but Kira is our star. Keep her happy and she keeps Wynters in business," Trevor shakes my shoulder.

I flush. "You're just being nice."

"Have you seen our quarterly projections since we

released your latest content strategy app? I'm not being nice. I'm giving credit where credit is due."

I am confident in my work, but it still feels nice to be valued so much. I don't know if I'd be as bashful about it if not for Orlie Wynters' intense gaze on me.

"Well, I'll leave you two to get acquainted. I'm going to make my rounds."

Before I can protest (although I'm not sure what I would say that wouldn't sound rude), Trevor lopes off in the direction of the CFO.

Leaving Orlie and me in an awkward silence.

"He's not lying, you know," Orlie is still staring at me . "He speaks very highly of you and your work."

I feel dwarfed by his height, like he could crush me. Although I can't say I'd mind being wrapped up in his arms. Beneath his jacket, I can only imagine there's a very well-chiseled chest.

Kira, this is your future boss. Stop it.

"I'm h-happy to hear that."

Orlie's jaw tenses. He's expecting me to say the next thing, but I'm at a complete loss for words. I can smell him from here. An expensive, strong cologne wafting off his body. Dark tobacco and amber.

I'm lightheaded.

"I think we've passed one another in the halls before. Forgive me if I've seemed standoffish, but I've been trying to prepare things for this...eventuality."

"It's no problem."

The corner of his mouth creeps up. "Besides, we all probably look the same to you."

I frown. "Huh?"

"In our suits and things. All of you in the tech department look like a circus compared to us with how freely you can dress."

My mouth drops. A *circus?*

I look down at my shirt.

What? Just because I wear stripes, he thinks he can stand there and call me a clown?

"It doesn't matter what you all wear, though. All we really need your brains. The rest of us are just..." He pulls on the front of his jacket and looks around. "Posturing."

I shake my head. I don't tend to care what people think of my appearance.

I've always been the smart girl. I've had glasses since I was three. I wasn't concerned with my beauty.

But hearing him dismissing me, reducing me to a brain, when I'm feeling all these strange sensations in my body is mortifying.

As if I haven't been stereotyped before because I'm quiet and prefer to be behind the scenes. I don't crave all eyes on me, don't need to be the loudest one in the room.

Sometimes I worry that may be the reason I've struggled to find the right man. It wasn't my priority when I was younger. But now that I'm the last single Solace sister, the clock is getting louder. I want to find that commitment. Someone to settle down with and start a family with when the time is right.

A companion. A peer. Someone to be there for me.

I straighten out my striped *circus* top. *That's one way to stand out.*

What does Orlie Wynters know about me anyway?

"Right. Well, I should get back to work. This meeting interrupted my flow."

Orlie raises an eyebrow but doesn't question me. "Of

course. I'm glad to officially make your acquaintance, Ms. Solace."

"Kira, just call me Kira," I'm able to mutter before rushing out of the conference room and back down to my basement office.

The second the door is closed behind me, I clap my hands over my head. "Motherfucker."

Orlie Wynters is nothing like his father. All it took was a two-minute conversation with him to realize as much. He's arrogant and pretentious and judgmental and –

Why didn't I say something? Being the star employee affords you certain luxuries, including mouthing off from time to time.

However, I'm too quiet for that. Too *nice*. I've kept my head down for years, even in my own family, not wanting to be the center of attention or cause any more drama than was already there.

Sometimes, though, that feels like a curse.

Because Orlie Wynters deserved a sassy reply for calling me and my team of techies "a circus." The executives are the real circus. Performing for everyone in their Valentino suits and smarmy smiles. We're the real deal.

However, not even in a different world would I have been able to say something to him.

As much as I don't want to admit it, Orlie Wynters took my breath away.

But I'm not going to let that get in the way of my work. Never in a million years.

2

———

ORLIE

PRESENT DAY

WHAT THE FUCK AM I DOING? I DON'T BELONG HERE.

I twist the glass of scotch on the table and stare at the ice cubes clinking together to avoid looking at the scene occurring on the dance floor.

Describing it as a scene makes it sound like it's some sort of chaos.

No. It's beautiful. It's just hard for me to look at it.

A romantic melody swoons through the air, some classic song by a crooner, perfect for weddings.

I force myself to pull my eyes up from the glass to look at Hunter and Amy swaying across the dance floor. The two of them are beautiful together, swaying and sliding in perfect rhythm. The way they look at each other makes it as if no one else in the room exists.

Fine. I'm jealous. I'll just come out and say it. I'm jealous of their happiness.

I swig the whisky and bid myself to put the jealousy aside and appreciate the happy couple. It's clear they adore each other.

My friendship with Hunter has grown exponentially

over the past few months, and I know he deserves it. More than that, his little girl deserves it.

Amy breaks her gaze from Hunter for only a moment to look over at little Jessica and waves the little girl over.

Jessica runs from her seat to join them on the dance floor.

Hunter scoops her up and the three of them embrace as the music reaches a trembling climax.

It's so lovely I think I might throw up.

Other couples start to waft onto the dance floor, joining their happiness. Amy's sisters, who I'm still trying to tell apart, are all joined by their significant others as they sway back and forth. They all seem so happy.

I keep my eyes on Drew for a long moment. But his happiness doesn't flinch from his face. From what I understand, Dana and him kind of tripped into an unplanned pregnancy. If that were me, I'd probably run the other way.

But the way he holds her in his arms and doesn't shy away from touching her swollen middle as they embrace makes it very clear he's head over heels with her.

Kira's the only one of them without a partner.

I've been sitting here feeling sorry for myself, but that must be a lot of pressure on her.

However, from what I know of Kira, she doesn't seem to ever think about anything but her work.

I glance around the room. Everyone is preoccupied with the goings on of the dance floor.

No one would miss me if I slipped out for a moment.

So, I get a refill of my scotch on the way out and then slip through the opening in the tent to breathe in the fresh ocean air.

It's a shame that everyone is hidden away in a tent when

the wedding is situated on a bluff overlooking the Pacific Ocean. Feels criminal to hide away from it.

I sip my fresh scotch and check the time on my Rolex. I could probably sneak away and no one would notice. Dinner service is over and done. All that's left is probably dancing, cake-cutting, bouquet-throwing...all the inane traditions that are supposed to usher in a marriage.

I take a few steps down the path back to the car park but stop when I spot someone out of the corner of my eye.

Kira Solace is sitting alone on a bench at the edge of the overlook. It was the pink flowers in her braided hair that caught my eye.

I swallow. There is no way she'd want to see her boss at her sister's wedding. We haven't said more than five words to each other since I got here.

But she's the only other person I really know here, other than the groom. Sure, the Solaces are welcoming and Hunter has introduced me to his friends, but Kira is the only one I'm *connected* to.

Which is sort of sad considering our connection is limited to contracts, codes, and coworkers.

Another sip of scotch.

Screw it. I'm going over there.

Measuring each step, I approach the bench, not wanting to scare her.

Her head twists just the slightest bit to look back at me. Not *directly* at me. Just enough to know I'm in her periphery.

I go to the other end of the bench and sit down. I don't even say "hi". I just sit.

The waves crash on the rocks below. A beautiful din. Out over the ocean, the sun is half-set, a golden yolk pooling across the horizon, streaking the sky with all sorts of unique shades of orange. Much better than having to be reminded of my loneliness inside the tent.

"Was Kennelworth satisfied?"

I look over at her almost shocked that she wants to talk work at her sister's wedding. But then I remember who we are to each other. There's nothing else to talk about when it comes to us.

"Yes, very much so."

Kira nods, eyes not leaving the view. "Good."

I open my mouth to say something more but stop.

Kira's radiance is...intoxicating. Even better than the sunset.

Her skin glows with warmth, her lips are blushed with a pigment that complements her skin perfectly, and her dark hair swept out of her face shows off the tight line of her cheekbone.

And I have to say I love that no matter the occasion, she still wears her black-framed glasses. Shows me she's uncompromising in all areas of her life.

I like that about her.

I lick of my lower lip. "I have to say, I'm much more excited to see what you'll be doing with the Leon Prep contract."

Kira smiles, glancing my way only briefly. "Me too. I've already got some ideas."

"I'm sure you do."

"Although, I'm kind of surprised you took the client on. It's not a particularly large contract." She frowns. "Surely, we're operating at a loss here."

I take another sip of my scotch. "Not everything needs to be a cash cow."

Kira hums. "That's good to hear you say."

"Is it?"

She tucks some loose hair behind her ear and shrugs. "It's nice to do things for the love of it. For the...for the potential change it could bring." Kira lifts her chocolatey brown eyes to me. "So, I'm thankful you chose me for the job."

"Of course. My dad said it best. You're the star."

"Which is why I'd imagine you'd put me on another major social app development or an analytics program. Not developing virtual classrooms."

I was a student at Leon Prep. So, when the headmaster approached me about developing virtual classrooms for their students to expand their accessibility for children with health needs, I was immediately intrigued. "You were the only person I thought of for the job," I say carefully.

Kira Solace is the most diligent worker I have. And while she's necessary to our bigger projects, the ones that have put food on my family's table for generations, I also need her where it counts. And this is a project that counts to me.

"Thank you, Orlie."

I strain to swallow without looking like a lunatic. Something about the way she says my name always puts a knot at the base of my throat.

Maybe because she says it so infrequently. Or maybe because the way she says it is so careful, almost like she treasures it.

Whatever it is, it does something to me.

We retreat back into silence. I said all we talk about is work, didn't I? It's just the way of the world when you're a CEO-to-be.

A year down in my transition to lead the helm at Wynters Group and I still feel like a foal taking its first few steps. I want to be able to prove myself to my father, but every time we have a meeting, I think he's about to pull the rug out from under me and tell me this was all just a joke and he's going to remain in charge of Wynters.

I'm trying, though. I really am. Just don't know if I'm trying the way I need to be.

God, Orlie, you're at a wedding. Do you really need to be thinking about work right now?

Truth is, my work is my life. It's everything to me.

Wynters Group is as much a part of me as the DNA in my blood. There is some sort of biological impulse in me to keep it going, just like many people feel compelled to have children. Wynters Group has replaced *those* impulses, thank God. No need to end up in some sort of loveless relationship with a child involved just because of one night of passion.

I'm not a robot...I have craved a loving connection before. I still do. But I can't be distracted. I need to prove to my father and to the world that I'm ready to take Wynters Group to the next level. The legacy needs to remain.

I suddenly feel Kira's eyes on me. I've been silent for too long. Keeping to myself.

I finish off the scotch and put the glass aside. Golden courage streams through my body.

No. I don't need to be thinking about work right now. One night off won't kill me.

I'm tired of being bitter. Focused.

Alone.

At least for tonight.

"Kira, would you like to dance?" It comes out as rushed and unplanned as a sneeze. However, just like a sneeze, you can't take it back and pretend like it didn't happen.

Kira doesn't respond, just turns to look at me.

For a second, I'm sure she's going to give me a piece of

her mind. About how inappropriate it would be for us to dance together. After all, I'm her boss.

But then she smiles.

Kira's smile is something I crave. A rare gem. Tight and true, creeping all the way into her eyes. "Sure. Let's do it."

Before I can even fathom what she's said, Kira gets up and floats past me and back toward the tent, her mossy green bridesmaid's dress trembling in the breeze. She stops suddenly and looks at me with a frown. "Are you coming?"

I've never gotten to my feet so fast. "Yes. Of course."

There's that smile again. It sends an electric shock through my body all the way down to my...

Stop it, Orlie. She's your employee.

Maybe after tonight, I can call Kira a little more than an employee. A friend.

But nothing more. Never more than that.

3

———

KIRA

The entire way to the dance floor, my heart threatens to leap out of my mouth.

What was he thinking? What am I thinking?

One dance. One friendly dance. Dances don't have to be romantic. They can be platonic and dutiful.

And Orlie is nothing if not platonic and dutiful.

However, out there on the bench, the things he said about giving me the project...however brief his explanation might be...

It was nice to hear that he cares about my work. Cares about how I feel about my work.

Orlie and I face each other on the dance floor. Thankfully, it's crowded enough that I don't think anyone could spot us and start to wonder if there's something more happening here than the reality of the situation.

A boss and employee sharing a dance at a wedding. A classic situation.

Stop lying to yourself, Kira.

"This is a good song to dance to," Orlie remarks.

I don't recognize the tune. But I'm surprised he does.

It's a romantic ballad with some singer plangently describing their love. I can't imagine Orlie listening to this song just for shits and giggles.

Orlie eyes me carefully, those dark eyes I first thought were black when I saw him. Turns out, they're as deep brown as they can be. Like bark made damp from the rain. Within the darkness, there are ridges of lighter brown and gold.

They're beautiful.

He takes a step toward me and rests his hand on my waist. I resist my entire body going ridge, praying he can't tell how his touch has sent shockwaves through me.

I have been harboring the knowledge that Orlie Wynters is beautiful for a year. Not just objectively beautiful, but beautiful to *me*. I have to resist staring at him, have to keep our conversations clipped and stifled so I don't start blabbing nonstop and show my cards to him.

Now his hand is on my waist and I'm not sure that my brain can hold out much longer.

Orlie takes my hand in his, holding it up between us. I quickly clasp his shoulder.

Act like you've done this before, Kira.

And then, Orlie starts to lead me in a casual step, side to side. Simple. He leads with purpose and tenderness.

I've seen him as a cold leader the whole year he's been working toward his goal of CEO. Now I realize he's been withholding that other side of him, showing us the dark side of his moon when there is a whole other half of it lit up by the sun.

Maybe that's a lot to garner just from the way he handles me while dancing. But it's my sister's wedding and I've had quite a bit of champagne. Let a girl live a little.

"You've got rhythm," he remarks. Objective. Fact.

"Have to when I'm trying at my keyboard all day."

Orlie smirks. "Is that so?"

I'm about to answer, but I'm cut off when Orlie gently pushes my waist, spinning me out away from him on the floor, keeping his hand tethered to mine.

I do my best to be graceful, however, trying not to fall off balance doesn't really lend itself to that.

"I wasn't ready!" I hiss back at him.

Orlie grins. *Grins!* I've never seen him grin in my life.

"Fine, you ready?"

He spins me back into his arms and this time, I'm prepared. My back lands against his chest as he curls his arms around me. I laugh.

"Not too bad, not too bad," he mutters right in my ear.

We continue to sway back and forth in this position. My face is so close to his. I could lean over and press a kiss against his smooth jaw.

I won't, though. That'd be inappropriate. It'd ruin everything.

However, the temptation is there, creeping all the way through my body.

I flip around to face him. Can't be caught in that trap for too long.

Orlie's hand settles on my waist once again, pulling me tighter to him this time, so tight that our bodies are nearly flush. *Nearly.* He has to remain professional too, after all.

"I hope having your boss at your sister's wedding isn't a buzzkill," he murmurs. His breath lands against my face, smelling bittersweet like the scotch he was drinking.

Having could be a double entendre, but knowing Orlie and his direct nature, I know it's not. Still though...to have Orlie Wynters. My head spins at the thought.

"Not at all," I say. "As long as you don't talk about how I looked in my dress to my coworkers."

He screws his forehead together. "You'd be upset if I told them you looked beautiful?"

My eyes widen despite myself. Did Orlie Wynters really just call me beautiful?

Orlie half shrugs. "Suit yourself. I won't say anything about how you looked tonight." Then, he leans in toward my ear to say something. He hesitates, though.

His breath lands against my ear and my body tingles with goosebumps.

"I mean it, though. You look beautiful tonight."

Be bold for once, Kira.

Fuck it. I press my body the rest of the way to his in thanks.

Our dance continues, except now I can feel all of him. And I mean *all* of him.

Either Orlie Wynters packs large or he's hard for me.

I think I might prefer the latter.

The rest of the world drifts away. I tuck my head up beside his, delicately tilting my nose and mouth toward his hair. Not a kiss. But now he can feel me too.

Our hips shuffle back and forth. Suddenly, I feel mine moving without thought or control, pressing into him.

From the nearly silent moan Orlie releases, I have my confirmation.

Orlie Wynters is hard for me.

And if I extrapolate that a bit, that means he wants to fuck me. Because he's attracted to me.

My head is spinning.

"I've never seen people dance to the 'Cha Cha Slide' like this."

I rip myself away from Orlie when I hear my sister Harley's voice.

"What?!" I nearly shout.

Harley throws her head back in laughter.

Sure enough, the 'Cha Cha Slide' is playing through the loudspeakers and everyone on the dance floor is doing the steps except for us two fools who hadn't even noticed the music had changed.

I glance at Orlie; he's red-faced, running his hand through his hair. He looks cute when he's embarrassed.

"Well, sorry to interrupt," my little sister says. Well, lies through her teeth, really. "But I need to pull Kira away for a moment. Sister stuff."

Orlie clears his throat and stands a little taller. "Of course. Don't let me keep you from that."

I give him a look of apology, but he doesn't seem to take it. That front he always puts on, like he's seeing through me, goes right back up. As if the dance didn't even happen.

So much for...whatever that was.

"Come on!" Harley grabs my hand and drags me out of the tent and back into the Pacific Ocean air.

It's dark now, the sun having set in the time Orlie and I were dancing.

Harley leads me down a path to a little clearing where my other three sisters stand together, looking like witches in the night with their ethereal dresses. Especially Amy whose lacy wedding dress seems ripped from a Victorian novel.

"Got her! She was *dancing*," Harley cries out.

"With whom?" Amy gasps with wide eyes.

I grab Harley by the arm. "I'll murder you."

Harley grins. "Orlie Wynters."

Great, now I have to plan the murder of my little sister. This isn't how I wanted the night to end, but...

"Ooooh! I always thought he was handsome," Gillian remarks.

"Can we hurry this up? I have to pee," Dana says, clutching the underside of her very pregnant stomach.

"You just peed!" Amy says.

"I have a baby sitting on my *bladder,* Amy!" my eldest sister hisses. Dana usually keeps it together for all of us as the eldest, the one who stepped up after our mother left. But pregnancy has been a whirlwind of hormones. I don't blame her for being edgier than normal.

Harley and I join our sisters, the five of us standing in a circle. "What are we doing?"

"I just wanted a moment. Just us girls," Amy says. She takes Dana and Gillian's hands and the rest of us follow suit. As kids, we would play Ring Around the Rosy just like this. "So much has changed in the past couple of years."

Harley squeezes my hand. Not sure if it's pity or an accident. Because all of my sisters have changed except for me.

Each of them is partnered up, blissed out in love. And it all happened so fast too. Two short years and we went from five single sisters to four partnered sisters and little old me.

Don't get me wrong, they worked to get there. Each of them came up against their own trials before they got to the tribulations.

I don't want that for me. An accident forcing me into understanding love. Sure, I want kids someday. But I want that conventional marriage, the way the old school rhyme is ordered. Love, marriage, baby carriage.

It's not that my sisters haven't found happiness in their ways. I'm so proud of all of them. Maybe feeling a little left out. But happy they've found what they were looking for.

No, it's because our mother had it the mixed up way.

She and Dad met in college, got pregnant, and then, for the next however many years, she pretended to be the mother who loved us.

Until she gave up.

I wonder what her life would have been like if she'd never met my dad. Would she have ever become a mother? Would they still be together?

These questions aren't helpful. But they're always there in the back of my mind.

Anyway, I'm the last single Solace sister. The last one living at home with Dad. And given how I'm married to my work, I'm not sure that will change any time soon.

"I know we all have our own families now," Amy says and then looks at me. "Our own lives."

Thanks for the correction, I think, bidding myself not to roll my eyes.

"But I will always be here for you," she says, her lower lip trembling. "First and foremost, you are my sisters. And I wouldn't be even a quarter – no – *a fifth* of the woman I am today without you."

The five of us all smile at one another, huddling closer together. We pull our interlocked hands into the center, like the center of a flower. Tears creep into the corners of my eyes, imagining each of my sisters falling away from this center point like petals.

We can say all we want that we will be here for each other. But life sometimes has a way of screwing that all up.

I have to trust them. Have to trust that they love me. That just because my life doesn't seem as full to them I'm not just an appendix.

God, I hope I'm not.

"I love you guys," Amy sniffles.

"We love you, Ames," Dana says and kisses the side of her head.

"There you all are!" Dad's voice cries from the mouth of the path. "Have I interrupted a moment?"

We all break apart and invite Dad into our embrace. "Just in time, Daddy," Amy says.

"You're crying again? Jeez, I thought you'd be cried out after your vows, but –"

"*Daddy!*"

Dad laughs and gives me a sidelong glance, winking my way. We have a special bond, ever since Amy moved next door to live with Hunter. We watch programs together and go for hikes. We sometimes talk in the middle of the night when neither of us can sleep.

And while Dad has never said it out loud, I know it would break his heart if I left.

So, while all my sisters move on, I'm stuck as the girl I've always been. Good, quiet Kira.

But I need more.

Something has to change.

4

———

ORLIE

My father is awful at golf.

Which makes our meetings couched as golf outings even more unbearable.

Listen, I love my father. For being a high-powered businessman he's been a very good father.

That doesn't mean I can't judge his golfing abilities.

"Fore!"

I want to pull my head into the collar of my polo like a turtle. "Dad, you don't have to yell 'fore' every time you hit the ball." *Especially not when you're putting.*

Dad stops mid-swing and turns around, a mischievous smile on his face. "I know. I just love how much it annoys you."

I sigh, leaning on my putter. "Are you going to make the shot or not?"

Dad lifts his head and looks into the sky, eyes squinching shut. It's a beautiful cloudless day. Perfect anywhere but LA. I was hoping he would come to his senses and we could have a lunch meeting instead of golf, but *nooo*. When my dad makes a plan, he sticks to it. Almost to a fault.

"What are you doing?"

"Slowing down, son. Taking it all in. Been working so hard these past few decades –"

I start to laugh. "Don't start with this."

He clutches his heart melodramatically. "I've missed so much in the world. I've taken it for granted."

"If you don't make the shot, I'll make it for you!"

Dad holds his hand up to stop me from moving an inch forward. "Don't rob me of these simple pleasures, son." He lines his putter up with the ball. "Fore!"

I cringe again.

Dad smacks the white ball with his putter, sending it whizzing it forward. It banks off the side of the hole, rounding the edge, and flies right back out to the other side of the green. We both stand there and stare at the golf ball that should have disappeared into the hole.

"Um –"

Dad's shoulders go rigid. "Don't. Say. Anything."

I put my hand over my mouth to stifle a laugh as he stomps over to the ball and silently sends it back to the hole. It slides right in without an issue.

"Don't worry, we can leave that first stroke off the scorecard," I say.

My father shakes his shock of gray hair out of his face and sighs. "No, that wouldn't be very honorable, would it?"

I roll my eyes. "Sure."

"Come on. Onto the next."

I follow Dad to the golf cart. He jumps in behind the wheel and starts off to the next hole.

"When are we going to do the meeting part of this meeting, Dad?" I ask, grabbing onto the roof as we bobble over the waving terrain. He drives like a maniac in these tiny things. He's wrecked not one, not two, but three of them on this very golf course.

Helps to be on the board when those kinds of things happen.

"I'm sorry, are you not having fun with your old man, Orlie?"

We hit a bump and I yelp.

"Oops, sorry."

"You know I'm not saying I'm not having fun. I'm just saying –'"

"I know you're a busy man. We both are. Like father like son." Dad smiles as he takes the cart down a slope. The next hole is in sight. "But fine, you want to talk business, let's talk." He turns the cart suddenly away from the hole and cruises across the course aimlessly.

I glance at some players we pass, wondering what they're thinking about the eccentric man driving the golf cart wherever he pleases. My dad has always been a bit on the wild side. I've taken more after my mom. Dower, serious, direct.

"I'm starting to think I might not be ready," he says carefully.

I blink. "What do you mean?"

"You know..." He shrugs one shoulder and then shakes his head. "Wynters Group has been my life. My whole life. I'm not sure I really need to leave. I like working. I always have."

My heart starts to race. I knew this would happen. I could tell just from the way my dad was extending the timelines of everything that needed to be done, edging my tenure as CEO further and further out of my grasp.

It's not that I'm some disgruntled son who wants to

overthrow my father's reign. It's not about that. It's about legacy. Honor.

I'm ready to do it. I don't have anything else in my life going for me except the business. If I can't pour myself into the role of CEO, then I'll need to find a fucking hobby. Crocheting? Knitting?

I don't know why fiber arts are the only hobbies I can come up with.

I just know Dad will never trust me again after I don't choose him. No matter how much I regret it, no matter how much I apologize. I don't know if he'll ever see me as strong enough as to make Wynters Group my life.

I'm evidently silent for too long. "Of course, this isn't a reflection of you, Orlando."

God, not the full name... Dad only uses my full name when he knows he's disappointing me. And I hate that he can *see* that he's disappointing me. I don't like to be pitied or felt sorry for.

"I think you've been doing a wonderful job preparing to fill my shoes. Although, you could afford to smile more."

"*Dad...*"

He chuckles and then pulls the cart into the gravel driveway outside the clubhouse. "Will you hate me if I don't go?" Dad asks, removing the keys.

It's not a real question. He doesn't even look at me to make sure I'm telling the truth. "I'd never hate you, Dad."

He smiles. "Then I did something right, I guess." Dad climbs out of the cart. "Well, what do you think? Bloody Marys on me, huh?"

I was prepared for a long business meeting where we talked about all the details of some of our plans moving forward. Instead, I've been conned into a Bloody Mary date with my dad. And I don't even like Bloody Marys.

We sit at the old wooden bar, sip the infernal red concoction, and split a soft pretzel between us. At least I can chase the taste of tomato and clam juice down with a delicious pretzel.

"So –" Dad pauses to swallow his pretzel, then dabs his buttery fingers on a napkin. "You're taking a vacation for a few weeks, right?"

I audibly sigh. "*Yes.*"

"Why do you sound so upset about it? I'd love a vacation."

"That's a lie and you know it." If he really wanted a vacation, he could follow through with the plan to make me CEO.

My dad claps his hand on my shoulder. "Vacation would be good for you. Clear your head."

"My head *is* clear."

"When do you head up?" Dad asks.

"Friday."

"Ah! Well, you'll have to send me pictures."

I smile sadly. Dad might be a pain in the ass sometimes, but we're all each other has got. And if I'm not sending him pictures, I know he isn't texting many other people about anything except work.

"Of course. I'll make you a whole scrapbook."

"Is that how you're going to pass the time? Yeesh. You ought to bring someone up there to keep you preoccupied."

I wince. "*Dad...*"

"Can't stay single forever, Orlie."

I check my watch.

"Getting tired of me?"

"No, I just have to meet Hunter to grab some things. I don't want to miss him before he heads up to Burbank, or else I'm going to be stuck in afternoon traffic."

"Mhm. Then you go. I'll finish this –" Dad grabs my unfinished Bloody Mary and starts to suck it down.

I laugh, giving him a pat on the back. "Take it easy, alright?"

I look at the bartender, an old guy named Fred I've known since I was a toddler. "You call him a car if he has too much Grey Goose, alright?"

Fred gives me a salute and I salute back.

Once I'm out of the clubhouse and in my car, I let out a sigh.

Where is the enjoyment in life? When are things going to change? Dad's not letting me and I can't seem to make it for myself. It's like I need to be struck by lightning or something.

As long as I survived it, maybe that wouldn't be so bad.

5

KIRA

I peruse the aisles of Quentin's Roadside Market, picking up various foodstuffs and ingredients I'd never eat if I wasn't in the middle of nowhere without another grocery store in sight.

I'm not trying to be fussy. I've just gotten used to my organic ingredients and health foods. Here, there are only national brand names. Boxes of Frosted Flakes and Nature Valley Granola Bars, jars of Jiff Peanut Butter, and don't even get me started on the produce.

Living in California, I'm spoiled.

But I'm about four hours away, in the mountains of Nevada, and everything is different out here.

That's why it's nice to get away. Be somewhere new, where I have to be out of my comfort zone and adapt.

This is what I do every time I start a new project. With my unlimited vacation time, I go away for a month or so and clear my head, get started on some abstract ideas, so that I can come back to the office reinvigorated and ready to take on the challenge.

After winding through the store. I make my game plan.

There are locally grown veggies which I snatch up, then I grab some frozen fruit, eggs, milk, meats, cheeses. Everything I can get my hands on. And right before I hit the cash register, I grab a pack of batteries.

For one, you can never have too many batteries.

For another, I have a brand new vibrator I'd like to try out with one of those sucking heads and it needs several batteries.

If I'm going to be up here for a whole month by myself, I'll need some way fun to pass the time, won't I?

Finally, time to check out. I realize halfway through the transaction I'm speaking with THE Quentin of Quentin's Roadside Market. He's a lovely man with a very broad smile and lots of questions.

Too bad I'm not good with questions like Amy or Harley. I always kind of shut down and give only the bare minimum of an answer.

I've always been shy. The glasses help with that. I can sort of hide behind them, see the world from behind the lenses rather than having to look at it with a naked eye.

It's the way I can protect myself. Also my superpower.

With bags weighed down with sugary cereal and canned veggies, I make it out to my trunk, managing to stuff the groceries in along with all my luggage. Then I hop back in and turn onto the main road to head up higher into the mountains.

In the cupholder, my phone starts to buzz. Amy's Facetiming me. I put the phone in the little cradle I have on the dash and answer. "Hello from the middle of nowhere!"

"Kira? Is that you? You're all fuzzy."

"I could say the same of you!" My eyes flick to the service bars on my phone. "I'm in the mountains. Got like two bars up here."

"That's more than I got!" she giggles. "How Inyo looking?"

I glance around at the towering trees. "Crisp from the summer. But beautiful. I don't even know how high up I am."

"Agh, I miss it there. I wish you would have let me come with you."

"You shouldn't have offered your husband's cabin if you were going to be disappointed I wanted to go alone," I say.

Amy squeals. "Husband! You said husband."

Cue the eye roll. "Yes, Amy. He's been your husband for like weeks now."

"Weeks is nothing! You'll understand when you're older."

I try not to take umbrage with the comment, but having your little sister experience much of life before you do is definitely not the best feeling in the world.

"Anyway, you know I'm just teasing you. I know you get out of town for your *inspiration*."

I smile. "Well, I'm still very grateful to Hunter for offering to let me use the cabin."

"Don't thank him. It was my idea."

"What was your idea?" I hear Hunter's voice off-camera.

"Honey! You're home!" Amy disappears for a second. The camera can't catch her fast movement. I glance at the service bars again.

Shit, I'm down to one.

"Hey, Ames, I should probably."

"Say 'hi'," I hear her whisper to Hunter.

Hunter ducks his head down to look in the camera, just a swatch of dark-colored hair and beard. "Hey, Kira."

I turn onto the road I marked earlier on my map. I knew

I'd lose out on service and didn't want to be stuck in the middle of nowhere with a cell phone with no service. "Hi, Hunter."

"Where – you –"

"Hey, you're starting to cut out," I say. "I think my service is –"

The road gets thinner and thinner until I hit the bridge Amy warned me about. Rickety, wooden, old. My heart starts pounding.

"She's at – cabin –"

Hunter starts to exclaim something, but the lack of service slows down his voice like he's a robot in slow motion.

"Guys? Hello?"

The screen is frozen on two blurred figures that look like they're in the middle of an argument.

"*Great.*" I hang up the call and then take a deep breath. "It's just a bridge, Kira, you can do this."

I pull the car forward the slowest it can go. As the tires creep over the bridge, I hear it strain beneath me. My god, how can this be legal?

I want to look out the window so badly to see how high up I am, but I also know that would kill me and I'd stall out right here and now, left to live the rest of my life on this bridge. "Just...keep...going."

Once my tires reach the lightly paved road on the other side of the bridge, I breathe the biggest sigh of relief I have ever breathed.

Maybe I *should* have invited Amy just so she had to do that drive instead of me. Because lord knows I'll be dreading doing it to go get more groceries.

For now, though, I put the bridge in the rearview, literally and figuratively. The road spirals a little bit before opening up onto a plot of land with a tall log cabin erected right in the center. It's beautiful, like something out of Architecture Digest. It's made up of dark, cherry wood, and there are plenty of windows giving a three-sixty view of the property and the Sierra Nevada in the distance.

Yeah, this is going to be good.

I get out of the car and start to unload things bit by bit. I have all the time in the world. And being out here in the wilderness certainly lends to that feeling. Trees are never in a hurry. Neither is the grass. Mountains. The animals.

Everything out here is completely different from the hubbub of LA and California.

I've needed to slow down.

Suddenly, there's a thumping sound. I look around for the source. I hear it again, this time more clearly. I shoot my gaze in the direction of the house.

Shit. Is someone here?

I shake it off. *Keep calm, Kira. There are going to be lots of noises out here you won't be able to identify, best to stay calm and –*

Thumping again. Louder this time. And clearly not nothing.

It's plenty possible some transient made camp out here. Although Amy mentioned the property was managed by some sort of company out here. It'd be strange if they didn't notice anything.

I don't keep weapons. But I did pick up a can of bear spray at Quentin's.

I feel the blood rush from my face when I realize it could be a bear. What kind of bears do they have out here? Grizzlies, surely.

God, this was a horrible idea, to come out here on my own, wasn't it?

I grab the bear spray and tiptoe toward the cabin. I

climb the steps and stand in front of the door. I peek in through one of the windows. Doesn't look like anyone is inside. I guess that would be a good sign if the alternative to a human wasn't a fucking bear.

I hear the sloshing of water from the back. Could it be a bear playing in the hot tub? Maybe they'll get footage on their security cameras and sell the video to America's Funniest Home Videos or something.

Thinking about a bear playing in a hot tub certainly alleviates my worry. But only for a moment.

I tiptoe down the veranda that encircles the building, closer and closer to the noise of shifting water.

I hear a deep sigh and freeze.

That's definitely the sigh of a person.

Don't panic. Don't panic. Don't –

I'm officially panicked. I'm not going to creep around here on pins and needles any longer. I need to know what the hell I'm up against. I round the corner of the house with my bear spray held up in front of me. "Stay back!" I shout. "I have a..."

My jaw falls when I find myself staring at Orlie Wynters. And not just any version of Orlie Wynters.

A very naked version.

And instead of looking away...I just stare at him. His chest is pale and looks like it's been sculpted by Michelangelo himself. The muscles and skin are taut, creeping down into a deep vee that frames his pelvis and then there's his...

"Kira!"

That snaps me out of my trance.

"What the –" Orlie scrambles and grabs a towel, encircling it around himself. "What the hell are you doing here?"

I open my mouth to speak, but my mouth is so dry no words happen. I rub my tongue against the roof of my mouth to gather some saliva. "I w-w-was just about to ask you the same thing."

Orlie clutches the towel around his waist, his chest heaving from the shock.

Why does his body have to be just as perfect as I imagined it?

"Let's go inside," he says in his stiff upper lip way, staring right through me as if I could be any of his employees, not one he danced with two weeks ago with a full erection in his pants. "Then we can talk."

6

———

ORLIE

"So, let me get this straight," I say, pacing the grand living room and trying not to think about how Kira stared at my cock earlier. "Amy offered you the cabin for a month and didn't tell Hunter. So, when Hunter offered it to me for a few weeks, he had no idea you'd be here?"

Kira is sitting on the edge of the couch with her hands on her thighs like she's a statue. "I believe that's the case, yes."

I run my hands over my face and through my hair. I'm dressed now, but I still feel completely naked. Talk about a breach of employer-employee privacy. "Well, this is just great."

"When did you get up here?" Kira asks.

"Last night."

"Ah."

We both are silent, waiting for the other to speak. Seems to be how things always are between us. Quiet.

"Well, I don't really feel like making the drive back today. And..." Kira finally lifts her gaze. "To be honest, I don't see any reason why I should leave."

I frown. "Well, me either."

"Between the two of us, it makes more sense that Hunter and Amy would let *me* use the cabin. I *am* family after all."

I resist arguing back that I'm her boss. That's not fair and it's also not something I want to harp on given the whole seeing me naked in the hot tub thing.

"Look, the last thing either of us wants right now is stress. That's why we're both out in the middle of nowhere avoiding people, right?"

Kira nods. "I guess so."

"Right, so..." I put my hands on my hips and tilt my head back. I might regret this. But I really don't see any other option unless I want to plan a whole other trip or head back to LA prematurely, which I know my father would hate.

"Look, this place is huge. We can make it work right?"

Kira recoils. "You want to stay here together?"

"Well, don't say it as if I disgust you."

"It's not that, it's –" Kira twists her lips to the side. "I can't imagine you'd want to spend your vacation being stuck here with me."

"Well, it's not about being stuck here with you, is it? We're both here. And we're both on vacation. But we're not on vacation together. Make sense?"

Kira sighs and leans back on the couch, finally sitting like a human instead of an android. "Fine. I guess we can make it work."

"You can take the master." I tend not to sleep in the main bedrooms out of respect. I can afford to fuck up the guest room. No ghosts there. "I haven't slept there, so –"

"I'm not sleeping in the bed where my sister has sex, Orlie. Gross."

"Well, the only other option is Jessica's room, so if you want to sleep in a bed shaped like a castle with a slide, then —"

"I want your room."

I clench my fists. A whole bespoke cabin in the mountains and Hunter only designed it to have three rooms. What kind of billionaire is he?

"Fine," I say. I'm not used to giving in to anyone except my father. But in this case, I want all the negotiations to be done with as swiftly as possible. I didn't come here to chat with Kira Solace, I came here to get away from everyone. That includes her, even if my thoughts have, from time to time, been visited by her and the way she felt in my arms at Hunter's wedding. "I will move my stuff. But you'll have to change the sheets."

Kira smiles. "I'm happy to. Thank you."

For someone so quiet, she certainly drives a hard bargain. "Yeah...whatever."

I wake up at seven in the morning to my whole body sweating. "What the..."

I sit up and wipe sweat off my brow, kicking off the covers and breathing a sigh of relief. It wasn't this hot when I went to bed, was it?

I get up and pull on a sweatshirt before heading out to the upstairs hall to check the thermostat.

Seventy-two degrees.

I know I definitely left it at sixty-five when I went to bed.

From downstairs, I can hear humming and the clatter of pots and pans.

Kira...

I crank it back down. It's not nearly that cold out to justify a balmy seventy-two.

I grit my teeth and walk down the stairs.

When I enter the kitchen, I'm hit with a sweltering burst of air. It's a mess. Kira has her back to me, bobbing back and forth, making some smooth concoction while eggs and bacon sizzle on the stove.

"Why is it so hot in here?" I ask.

Kira doesn't respond. She sings a lyric to a song and then shakes her hips.

"Hello?"

Again, she doesn't respond. I peer at her a bit closer. Must have headphones in.

I stomp over to her. "Kira!"

Kira sees me in her periphery and leaps out of her skin. She pulls out her earbuds. "Orlie! You scared me!"

"Why was it seventy-two degrees when I woke up?"

Kira takes a couple of deep breaths, still trying to shake the shock. "Because I was cold last night."

"You changed it from sixty-five to seventy-two. That's seven degrees."

She tends to the eggs and bacon with a spatula. "I know basic math, thanks."

"That's too hot."

"I like to not turn into an ice cube when I'm sleeping. You know, it's a self-preservation thing." She goes to the green concoction and takes a sip. Her face curls. One of those green smoothies everyone claims to like but they actually just taste like dirt.

"Well, I like to be at a logical, comfortable temperature," I say.

Kira shrugs. "I'll put it on seventy tomorrow night."

"No, not seventy. Sixty-five is a perfectly fine temperature for our purposes."

Kira slides the eggs and bacon onto the plate. I have to admit it looks pretty good. Too bad she doesn't have extra for me to snag a bite.

"It's not perfect for our purposes seeing as I've just told you I can't sleep when it's sixty-five."

I watch her as she goes to sit down in the breakfast nook by the window and starts scrolling on her phone before taking a bite of her food.

"You didn't say you couldn't sleep, you just said –"

"I can't sleep if it's a pin under sixty-nine. And that's my final offer."

For someone who spends all her time in the basement of Wynters Corp writing code, she clearly drives a hard bargain. If I disliked her more, I'd probably fight harder. "I can do sixty-nine."

The slightest flush creeps up in her cheeks. "Um. Great."

I resist smiling. Does Kira Solace's mind belong in the gutter? If so, I'd like to see what else makes her blush.

"Is that all? I have to do my New York Times Crossword."

So do I. But I usually do it lying in bed under the covers rather than in front of a full breakfast at seven in the morning.

"Yes, that's all."

"Great. Thanks for the talk, Mr. Wynters." She flings my title at me like a stone from a slingshot. It hits me right in the sternum. I don't like it. Feels false. Feels...

Feels like she doesn't like me.

But you know what? That's just fine. We don't have to

like each other. For the next few weeks, we're just room-mates on vacation and nothing more.

I can do that. Even if it has to be sixty-nine degrees.

Our first day at the cabin is relatively uneventful mostly because we avoid each other as much as possible. Kira barely leaves her room after her breakfast. I almost feel bad for admonishing her about the temperature until I remember how hot I was waking up in the morning.

When I wake up on the second day, the temperature is at the agreed-upon sixty-nine degrees. I might be an adult, but I'm still a man. It's hard to resist a chuckle at the six and the nine side by side.

Kira seems more active today. I've allowed her to commandeer the office on the first floor seeing as she's actually here to do work while I'm here pretending *not* to do work. Although, I have given myself a break from attending to emails to read.

I've been working through all of Proust slowly but surely over the past few years and have found a wonderful little spot out on the veranda overlooking the backyard. I ignore the bubbling hot tub in my periphery so as not to dredge up the shame of Kira's arrival.

Lost in the prose, I don't even notice Kira stepping out on the veranda until she clears her throat.

"*Ehem.*"

"Mm?" I glance her way and then look back at the words on the page. "What?"

"You're outside."

I furrow my brow and place my bookmark between the

pages. Clearly, something is going on. "Yes, it does appear that way, doesn't it?"

"If you're *outside*, why are all the lights on *inside*?" Kira asks. "For that matter, why are any lights on in the common spaces when it's noon on a cloudless summer day?"

I peek into the window behind me and see that, indeed, the warm yellow lights are on. At night, they fill the living room with a very pleasant glow. During the day, they're eaten up by the clear white light streaming in through the skylights.

"Ah. Sorry about that. Must have forgotten."

Kira doesn't move a muscle. Her usually pleasant, if not stoic, countenance is weighed down by her bending lips. "I didn't know billionaires contributed to climate change in their personal lives too."

I scoff. "Beg your pardon?"

Her eyes skitter away from me. "I'm just saying. It's wasteful."

Kira doesn't get to back out that easily, not when she's just accused me of being wasteful based on my socioeconomic status. "I forgot that you are literally perfect and never make mistakes. My fault."

"That's not what I'm saying."

"Then why are you accusing me of being a *wasteful billionaire?* We deal with tech, not oil or –"

"Tech can be wasteful! Being plugged in all the time. I mean, crypto is responsible for one percent of the world's –"

"Kira, I assure you that me leaving a light on is very negligible in its impact on climate change."

She grunts in frustration. For a moment, it's almost cute, the way her creaseless forehead deepens in the middle. *Almost.*

"You're impossible."

"Need I remind you that *you're* the one who wanted to waste energy on making the house as hot as the equator."

Kira crosses her arms over her chest. "Fine. That's fair."

I merely blink at her. I didn't expect her to back down so easily. Or be willing to accept her own fault. When it comes to the people I deal with on a day-to-day basis, admitting you're wrong is seen as a weakness. But I don't see that as a weakness in Kira.

I see that as a strength.

"Well, try not to leave the lights on, alright?" she says softly, adjusting her glasses.

"I'll do my best not to forget."

Kira stares at me for a prolonged moment, almost like her eyes are trying to see my soul. I shift uncomfortably in my seat. Don't want anyone seeing *that*.

"Anyway, I'll let you get back to your reading." She slips back inside before I can utter a thank you.

When I open the book again, I can't seem to focus on the words. They're all mushing together, swirling through my head. There is no meaning behind them.

I give up on the book and look out across the property. Overhead the mountains cut through the sky like giants.

And for just that one second, I wish someone was here to enjoy the view with me.

Maybe even Kira.

7

———

KIRA

"*Mmph.*"

My ears perk up when Orlie sighs from the kitchen. I knew I should have made sure to close the office door all the way because now I can hear him padding and clinking around.

"*Mmph.*"

And *sighing.*

A clatter of a pan, the running of water. Too much frenetic noise to remain focused on my work.

I lean back in my chair and close my eyes. *Deep breath.*

"You are water," I murmur to myself. "You exist in all states. You can persevere in all climates. You will –"

My meditative mantras I picked up from Gillian are interrupted by another sigh, accompanied by a soft, "Fuck."

I snap my eyes back open as my lower half feels a shock out of my control. The way Orlie's mouth wrapped around that word was so devastatingly perfect, it was as if I was watching an erotic film.

Except given the continued clatter, I'm very sure that "fuck" was out of frustration.

I get up to close the office door but decide instead to see what's bothering him. Maybe I can help and drive him to do literally *anything* else.

I go into the kitchen to find Orlie at the sink, scrubbing a pot I used earlier to make a box of mac and cheese. "Oh, that's mine, I'll do it."

Orlie whips his head around and glares at me. "I've got it."

Yikes. I creep closer to him. "Seriously, Orlie, I was going to –"

"Just let me do it," he says.

"I don't feel comfortable with you washing my dishes, I'll –"

"For fuck's sake, Kira, I said I'll do it."

I freeze right where I stand.

Please don't speak to me like that.

I wish I could say it aloud. But telling people how to treat me has never been my forte.

As if sensing my displeasure, Orlie sighs and finally turns to face me. "Look, I really hate having dishes in the sink. I don't like cooking in a dirty kitchen."

I chew on the inside of my cheek. "You could just throw it in the dishwasher."

"That won't get all the caked-on...cheese gunk that you've let calcify onto the pot." He gags at the subject.

"Don't talk about my food as if I somehow disgust you," I say.

Orlie rolls his eyes. "When did I ever say that?"

I ignore him and stomp over to join him in front of the sink. I rip the pot out of his hands, our fingers connecting for the briefest moment that sends my head spinning. "I'll do it."

Orlie grabs it back. "I said *I'll* do it."

Oh, we're playing this game, are we? "No, I wouldn't want to make you vomit while cleaning *my* dishes."

"I'd hate to distract you from your work in order to show some common decency in the kitchen," Orlie snaps back.

We tug back and forth on the pot, zipping quips at each other until I grab the soapy handle and the pot tumbles down into the sink, hot water and soap suds spring up at us.

We both gasp and jump away. The front of my shirt is soaked.

As is the crotch of Orlie's pants.

I hold my lips together, attempting not to laugh. But his dampened khaki shorts make it look like he's just –

"Don't you dare laugh."

I cover my mouth. Somehow, his pointing it out makes it even funnier.

"Kira."

I am shaking from holding my laughter back. I close my eyes tight, tears springing up at the corners.

"You're laughing!"

"I'm sorry!" I cry out, hiccupping laughs. "But you look like you peed yourself!"

Orlie flushes, and for the briefest second, the corners of his lips turn upward. He thinks it's funny too.

"It's your fault."

"Oh, come on, you were being stubborn. You should have just let me wash the pot."

I skootch in next to him, lightly bumping my hip against his to move him out of the way.

"Well, if I look like I peed myself, you look like you entered a wet T-shirt contest."

I freeze mid-scrub of the pot. "I suppose I do."

I don't dare look at Orlie. Nor do I look down at my shirt. I'm not wearing a bra. I'm on vacation. And I don't want to know what he's seeing. If he can see the contours of my breasts more clearly than ever or even worse *my nipples.*

Orlie clears his throat. "Um, anyway –"

"Sorry about the dishes," I say. "It won't happen again." And I mean it. Because there's no way I'm going to let Orlie Wynters enter me in a wet T-shirt contest again.

———

Our fourth day at the cabin and I haven't dared to leave my room since Orlie stomped into my room without knocking to ask me if I'd eaten his yogurt.

What he got in return was not only an answer but an eyeful of me bent over my suitcase, naked, deciding what to wear.

Again, I'd apparently left the door cracked. Need to quit that habit, it's getting me into very strange predicaments.

Orlie shouted loudly in shock and shielded the view with his hand almost immediately. Better than me after I stared at his flaccid dick when he'd emerged from the hot tub just a few days earlier. "You're naked!"

"Of course I'm naked! This is my room!"

Orlie ducked out of the room and asked his question through the crack in the door to which I snorted in laughter and said, "Me, eat plain yogurt? Dream on."

"Then where did it go?"

"I don't know. Have you been sleep-eating by any chance?" I ask.

Orlie paused.

"Wait. Do you sleep-eat?!"

"None of your business!"

I smiled to myself. Of all the weird habits to have, that's a pretty cute one.

"Anyway, sorry about the..."

"Yeah. Guess we're even."

Based on Orlie's lack of reply, I regretted saying it almost immediately, and the mortification of reminding him of how I'd found him naked climbing out of the hot tub sent me into a spiral. I abandoned all work for the day and have been watching home renovation shows on my laptop.

With a few breaks sprinkled in for...physical recreation in the form of playing with my new vibrator.

And *no*, I wasn't thinking of Orlie, how dare you even suggest such a thing?

Yes, I'm obviously lying.

Instead of meals, I've been binging on the snacks I kept in my backpack for the trip up here. But by dinner time, I know that raw almonds, beef jerky, and protein bars aren't going to cut it.

I sneak out of my bedroom with hopes of avoiding Orlie at all costs, but the second I do, I am hit with the wonderful aroma of garlic and onions. He must be cooking. And against my better judgment, I want to see what he's making.

As I walk down the stairs to the foyer, I hear some crinkling jazz music playing. The old turntable is spinning and, from the album cover, it looks to be a Miles Davis. I smile. That feels very Orlie Wynters.

I go to the doorway of the kitchen. Orlie is chopping vegetables at the kitchen island, an apron hanging around his neck. It's clean and white, save for streaks of bright pink across the belly. He looks up at me from his work for only a moment, but in that moment, he is the hottest thing in the world. Those dark, captivating eyes, the curious smile. "Hi, Kira."

"Hi."

Orlie doesn't say anything else, instead scooping up some herbs on the edge of his knife and dumping them into a cast iron skillet.

"What are you...what are you making?"

"Just some chicken piccata with broccoli rabe and a beet and goat cheese salad," he says plainly, wiping his hands off on the apron.

"Ah, that explains the pink, then."

Orlie looks down at his front. "Beets are messy," he says matter-of-factly.

"Yeah, looks like it." I'm starting to salivate. "It smells good in here."

"Thank you."

"I didn't know you could cook."

He shakes his head. "I cook enough to feed myself. I don't know if I *know how* to cook."

"You're talking to the girl who made boxed mac and cheese yesterday." No wonder he found it so abhorrent. This guy casually makes chicken piccata.

Orlie chuckles. "Yes, well, I'll just say the boxed stuff isn't for me. I don't judge anyone else's taste, though. Different strokes for different folks, as it were."

I tilt my head up against the doorframe. For a split second, I'm filled with a nostalgia that doesn't exist. Nostalgia for something in the future. Does that happen to people?

Well, in this future, I imagine Orlie whipping up dinner for a table where all the places are set. The fancy version for him and his wife and maybe some fancy, elevated mac and cheese that doesn't come from a box for the little ones.

I'm not sure if that's a future he sees for himself. Or

whether he'd even be capable of softening enough for that. But it's a beautiful image.

"You want to join me?"

I shake off my haze. "Hm?"

"For dinner."

"Oh. Sure." I take a step into the kitchen carefully. "Although I don't want to get in your way while I heat up a cup-a-noodle."

Orlie's lips twist up, "What in god's name is cup-a-noodle?"

I giggle. "You don't want to know."

He shakes his head. "No, Kira, I meant...would you like to have the dinner that I am cooking with me?"

My eyes widen. "Oh."

"Or even –" He swallows and hurriedly attends to something boiling over on the stove. "You don't even have to join me. You could just have some."

"I'd hate to impose when you're working so hard and I'm just mooching."

Orlie flips back around, his usually perfectly coiffed dark hair coming loose. Breathless with a smile. "It's not mooching if I offered. Plus, there's too much here for just one person."

I smile and creep over to the island and pull open the drawers for the placemats. "Alright. I'll set the table."

He runs his hand through his hair. "Sounds perfect."

My heart thuds in my chest.

By the time Orlie has set my plate full of the most delicious-looking, vibrant food I've ever seen in front of me, I can't help but feel that this dinner is a little bit like a date. Maybe date adjacent.

As he pours a full-bodied red wine into my glass, giving me a soft smile as he does so, I think date adjacent might just be heaven.

"Thank you," I say. "This looks divine."

Orlie settles into the seat across from me and removes his apron with a sigh of triumph. "You're very welcome. Please, eat."

My eyes have devoured the whole plate three times over already, so by the time I actually lift my fork to dig in, I don't know where to start.

"Where did you learn to cook like this?"

Orlie grabs for his wine first, pausing before he takes a sip. "My grandmother. When Dad was working too much, I'd spend sometimes weeks, months on end with her. And if you think this is any good, her food is ten times better."

"She still cooks?"

"If you go over just to say hello, she'll make you have a five-course meal. She's trained in the French style."

"You were a lucky kid, then."

Orlie snorts. "Tell that to the six-year-old me who was forced to eat *escargot*."

I laugh and then go back to my plate, still unsure where to stab my fork first.

"Um, sorry, we should cheers first, huh?"

I drop my fork with a clatter. "I – oh – yes." I grab my wine so harshly it nearly flies out of the glass. "Sorry, I'm excited."

"That's not something to be sorry for."

I lift my glass to meet Orlie's. "What are we cheersing to?"

Orlie smirks. "Not killing each other by the end of this?"

"Not walking in on each other naked again?" I follow up.

"Both formidable things to cheers to. Perfect. To all of that, then."

We clink our glasses together, solidifying our agreement. No killing, no nudity. Sounds like a PG movie.

I take a sip of the wine. Warm and luscious on my tongue, curling down my throat and into my belly. I feel warm all over with just one sip. Heaven.

"It's good, isn't it?"

"Mm, yes. Where'd you get it?" I reach for the bottle on the table and spin it toward me. The label reads Wynters Winery. I narrow my eyes at him. "Your family owns a winery?"

Orlie shrugs as if all families have wineries. "My grand-mother's venture."

"This grandmother of yours sounds like quite the lady."

"She is." Orlie cuts into his chicken piccata and takes a bite. His eyes flutter shut. "Mmm..."

I can imagine his eyes fluttering shut for other reasons than that.

Kira, get it together.

I follow suit and take a bite. And then another. And then another. Everything tastes *divine* from the tangy goat cheese to the spicy capers. Even the broccoli rabe is delectable. "This is amazing."

"Don't worry if you finish something. There's more."

I get a second helping of everything, including the wine. And despite the heavy meal, the wine is going right to my head. It's all starting to sink in. I'm in a cabin in the middle of nowhere with Orlie Wynters. My boss. And the man I've had a slightly inappropriate crush on for over a year.

I pause after a sip of wine and take him in. Whereas I ravenously devoured my first helping, Orlie is still working through his with delicate precision. He looks as focused and determined as he does when leading a big meeting.

I've always judged him for being so serious. Maybe that's just Orlie.

Maybe that's what I like about him after all.

"You're a good dancer."

Holy shit, did I just say that?

Orlie stops midchew and looks at me. "Where did that come from?"

I slide my hands over my cheeks. They're so warm. If it weren't for the wine, I'd be running a fever.

Can't take it back, Kira. Out with it.

"I never told you. After the wedding. But you're a very good dancer."

Orlie's seriousness splits and something tugs at the corner of his mouth. "Thank you, Kira. So are you."

"No, I'm fine. But you, you're very good."

Okay, now you're laying it on a little thick.

Orlie eyes me from across the table.

It's not very big and if I let my impulses get the better of me, I could lunge across and grab him by the back of the neck and lay one on him right now. But my impulses won't win. I, Kira Solace, am always in control of them.

I watch him take a calculated sip of wine, then swish the glass around so the bowl is tinted with red. "Why wait until now to tell me?"

"Well, there's never been a good moment. At work, you know, it's all —"

"So, you've been thinking about it."

I didn't know it was possible to go pale and blush at the same time, but my body is all sorts of messed up over that comment. I wouldn't be surprised if I spontaneously combusted too.

"You've been thinking about dancing with me."

I can't hold his gaze for very long. It's like there are magnets in his eyes attaching to my every word, trying to pull them from my mouth.

Must...be...strong.

"You know, since you cooked, I'll clean. How about that, huh?" I shoot up from my chair and collect the plates on my side of the table.

"Kira –"

"No, I know you think I'm not very good at it, but just wait. I'll make up for that crusty pot, you'll see."

As I rush over to the sink, I hear Orlie get up from his chair. My brain screams, "No! Stay away," but my body is begging, "Yes...come closer."

"I have no doubt you would do an amazing job, but –"

"Thank you again, for dinner. Delicious. Ha! I don't think there are any leftovers. I ate so –"

I feel Orlie's hand on my shoulder. He yanks me away from the sink, spinning me toward him. I press myself up against the sink, but there's nowhere for me to go. He's practically on top of me. Only an inch away.

His eyes examine every inch of my face. And I'm in such shock that I can't act on any single impulse I stifled while I was sitting across from him at the dinner table.

Orlie's hips brush up against mine. He bends his neck down to look into my eyes.

"D-dishes won't clean themselves," I stutter.

He shakes his head. "Leave it."

Without another word, Orlie slides his hand around the

base of my skull and pulls me into a deep kiss. My body starts to go limp until his hips increase the pressure against mine. I grab onto the collar of his shirt to keep from crumpling into a ball of nothingness. A groan slides from his mouth into mine.

I'm kissing Orlie Wynters.

I'm kissing *my boss.*

And while I know I should stop this right here and now. I don't want to.

Actually, I can't.

Orlie tears his lips away from mine, but his face is still so close I can feel his deep, heaving breaths on my cheeks.

"I've been thinking about that dance with you too."

Before I can respond, he locks me into another kiss.

"Been thinking about how close we were that night."

Another.

"How I could have kissed you right there."

Another.

"Claimed you."

Orlie grabs at my thighs, pressing our pelvises together without relenting. I can feel his thick hardness, just like I did at the wedding. Except now, we're alone. Now, there's no reason to hold back.

"You feel that? You feel what you do to me?"

I blink my eyes open, but Orlie is obscured by the fog on my lenses. I wish I could see that desperation painted across his face just as well as I can feel it in his pants.

"It's not fair, Kira. Not at all."

Fuck holding back. Orlie has made it clear he isn't going to. So, I won't either. I lunge for him, leaping into his arms and smashing my lips onto his. Orlie stumbles back against the island but manages to stay balanced, keeping me in his arms.

I devour his lips, I nip at his neck, I relish the salty taste of his skin.

"Oh my fucking god…" he whimpers.

"If you want me so bad," I growl into his ear, "What are you going to do about it?"

A laugh bubbles out of Orlie's gut, dark and thick. I want to live in that laugh, full of anticipation and potential. Terrifying and tempting me at the exact same time.

"Well, if you'd let me, I'd like to fuck you absolutely senseless."

I kiss him again, cupping his cheeks in my hands. Though he's clean-shaven, I can feel the buds of his facial hair under my hands, a delicate prickle.

"I think that can be arranged."

Orlie smiles.

"Although…" I kiss him. "I didn't bring condoms with me. You know, thinking this was a solo trip and all."

"I'm surprised Kira Solace doesn't come prepared at all times."

I laugh nervously. "Well, spur-of-the-moment sexcapades aren't as common in my life as you may think." I push my glasses up the bridge of my nose for emphasis.

Orlie laughs, running his hands up my thighs. I haven't worried he might drop me for even a second. He is strong and steady. "Well, you don't have to worry because I actually – um – I had a vasectomy a couple of years back. So… Yeah. You don't really have to worry about the pregnancy thing."

There goes that weird moment earlier when I was watching him in the kitchen, thinking about his little family. I suppose there are many other ways to make a family, but the fact he got his tubes tied makes it seem like that's a thing he firmly wouldn't want.

"And I've been tested. Recently."

"Same. Me too. I'm clean."

"Great."

"Great."

And with all the nitty gritty out of the way, the depravity commences once more.

Orlie switches us around again, propping me up on the edge of the counter. His hands tickle at the waistband of my shorts. "God, I want you right now…"

"Have me right now, then."

"You sure?" He leans over me until I have no choice but to lay back on the kitchen island. "You won't think less of me for taking you in the kitchen?"

"No, if anything, it makes me excited how badly you want me."

Orlie has never looked more relaxed in his life as he stands before me, a sly smile on his lips and his eyes half-shuttered with lust. *For me.* He rips open the closure on my shorts and pulls them down, leaving my bottom half almost completely exposed except for my underwear.

"Believe me. I *need* you. Badly."

I sigh.

"And…" Orlie pushes my T-shirt up and presses a kiss to my belly button. "For the record…"

"Yes?" I say, starting to squirm.

He continues a line of kisses down to my thighs. My center is aching for his lips and he knows it. And just before he finally gives me what I'm after, he meets my gaze, eyes sparkling. "I love your glasses."

That's *not* what I was expecting. So much so that I start to laugh; the laugh is cut short when Orlie runs his tongue along the seam of my vulva. I buck without warning. He wraps his arms around my thighs and starts to caress my pussy with his lips, eating me like I'm some delectable dessert.

I slide my fingers through his hair and moan out his name.

Orlie's tongue dips out of me and again licks me stem to stern, engulfing my clit in a tense band of pressure.

I gasp for air, my back lifting off the marble countertop. "Fuck, you can't – you can't –"

Orlie tears his mouth off me. "Can't? Should I stop?"

"No, no, it feels so good. Too good." I sit up and take off my glasses to rub my eyes.

Orlie puts his hands beside my hips. "Kira…" he whispers, mouth near my ear. "You deserve to feel *amazing*."

Who is this man and what has he done with my robot of a boss, Orlie Wynters? Has this been brewing underneath the surface of our relationship all along? Or does he just know the right things to say?

Orlie kisses my temple. "I'll stop if it's too much."

"No, no, don't stop," I say, grabbing onto his collar.

His face shifts toward mine. Lips coated in my essence. "Please don't stop."

Orlie smiles. "Let me take you to the bedroom."

Without another word, Orlie scoops me up in his arms as if he's carrying a bride across a threshold, except his bride is me and she's not wearing pants. It feels as though the entire way, we are entangled in kiss after kiss. Not for a second am I worried he might trip.

When we make it to my room, Orlie lays me out on the bed and climbs on top of me without hesitation. We work the rest of our clothes off until we're both naked and entwined together in all ways except for where it really matters.

Orlie's lips on mine are heavenly, no matter how hard

he kisses me. I can already feel the bruises forming on my bitten lips. A reminder for tomorrow of how badly he wanted me.

"I want to be inside you."

"What are you waiting for?" I ask, pushing my hips up against his.

Orlie adjusts himself at my entrance and pushes his hips forward inch by inch, paying attention to the way my breathing changes.

"You okay?" he grunts.

Sparks alternate with pangs of stretching. It's been a long time since someone has been inside me. And no one has ever been inside of me bare. His naked cock running up against my inner sanctum is unlike anything I've ever felt before. "Mmm...yeah."

"I'll go slow at first," he whispers against my jaw.

"Don't have to," I reply and jolt my hips again.

Orlie whines like an injured animal. He thrusts into me, creating a beautiful rhythm that leaves me breathless. I cling to him, scratching my nails up his back, moaning into his neck. "Feels...so good."

He laughs weakly. Concentrated.

His hands slide up under the pillows, going to grip the edge of the mattress, but he stops. "What's..."

As he withdraws his hand and I see what's clutched in his fist, I flush down the length of my entire body. "Oh god, that's —"

"Did you bring a toy?" Orlie says, a lopsided smile on his face as he holds up the pink vibrator.

I can't find the words to respond. There's no way to excuse my way out of this. After all, he's found a vibrator in my bed. That's pretty incriminating evidence.

"I've never seen one like this before," he says.

"Why are you smiling like that?"

Orlie laughs, throwing back the sweaty pieces of his hair out of his eyes.

"Because it's so sexy to know that you touch yourself."

I'm melting. I'm fully melting the same way Orlie does when the temperature is over seventy degrees at night. "It's a sucking vibrator. That part goes on the clit."

His eyes widen, a flash of fire alighting the dark brown. "Really?"

"Yes, now –" I reach for it, but he jerks it out of my reach. "Orlie!"

"Why are you embarrassed?"

I try to grab it again, but still, I cannot manage to grasp it. "Because you're inside me and now you're asking for a QVC demonstration of –"

I'm interrupted by the buzzing sound of the vibrator. I gulp.

Orlie's eyes meet mine. Though I feel tremendously safe here in his arms, there's a darkness in his eyes. It's so undeniably sexy and makes my body even warmer than it already is.

He lowers his mouth to my ear and slides the vibrator down the length of my body to my hip. "Can I use it on you, Kira?"

"Uh...uh-huh."

I can feel the smile move across his mouth just as I feel the vibrator move from my hip to my pubic bone. Orlie lifts himself to make space for the toy, then lowers it toward my center. He suddenly bucks, gasping. "Oh god –"

"Did it hit you?"

He laughs, trying to recover. "Yeah, that's intense."

I take his wrist and guide the vibrator over my clit. The

vacuum latches on; my entire body curls and a moan strains out of my mouth.

"Fuck, you're so hot," he mutters.

As Orlie thrusts again, I can't breathe, overwhelmed with the sensations from inside and out. I try to speak, but I can't. It just comes out garbled. Everything feels so good. I'm sure I won't last long.

"Your eyes..."

Rolling back, in my head. And my legs are shaking, vibrating with the onslaught of pleasure I'm feeling.

"God, you're beautiful."

In a moment of clarity, I wrap my legs around his waist, grab onto his ass, and pull his entire body onto mine. Orlie grunts, the vibrations from the toy now up against the base of his cock. "Keep going," I beg. "Feel it with me."

Orlie's whole self is sheathed within me, so deeply he can only make shallow thrusts. That's all I need, though, because the toy is pulsing around my clit, ready to pull the orgasm out as soon as I allow it.

I want Orlie to come with me, though. I want to hear him fall before me.

"Oh, god," he says. "It's too intense, I can't –"

"Come inside me, Orlie. Come for me."

"No, no, no, it's too soon, it's –"

I grab a handful of his hair and position his head so we can look into each other's eyes. "You come for me right now, please, please, *please*. I need it," I say through clenched teeth.

Orlie's resistance is futile; the second I see the terror of his unavoidable orgasm flick through his eyes, my body shudders beneath him, giving in to the growing pressure in my clitoris and his depth. Orlie searches for something to grab, hands puttering about the pillows. He plows as deeply as he can into me and releases, warmth trickling inside me. Cum without the seed. Still feels as good as I've always imagined. Just doesn't have that same sort of trembling anxiety that we've made a mistake.

None of this could possibly have been a mistake.

"Off," I whisper hurriedly. The toy is starting to become too intense. "Take it off or I'll –" My body shakes again, another, lesser orgasm. "Shit, oh, mm –"

Orlie lets me ride it out, then turns off the toy and puts it to the side. Collapsing over me, he lets out the most plea-sured sigh and presses a kiss to my neck. A tender one.

I rub his back as his member ebbs to its usual state, enjoying the sheen of sweat against my fingertips.

Sadly, he eventually has to roll off of me to come back down to earth.

"Fuck," he mutters into his hands, threading his fingers back through his hair. "That was..." Orlie looks at me. Probably looking for a clue of how I'm feeling about this.

"Really good," I confirm.

"Yeah, good. I'm glad you felt that way because that was..." A smile settles in his mouth. One of wonder. Some-thing I've never seen on his face before. Not when he's trying to posture and be the big, bad wolf, Orlie Wynters, bossing us all around. Here in bed with me, he has softened into something more vulnerable.

I want to keep this version with me. It's such a gift.

"That was fucking amazing," he finishes.

"I'm glad you think so."

Orlie gets up on his elbow and wraps his hand around my waist. Dropping into silence, his eyes scan the length of my body, up and down, until finally settling his eyes in mine.

I hold my breath. The enigma behind his eyes is unknowable.

"You're a total surprise, Kira."

"How do you mean?"

He shakes his head, smile growing wider. "I don't really know."

I laugh, taking his head in my hands and drawing him into a long kiss. Orlie gives in to me, humming into my mouth with delight.

When the kiss breaks, Orlie doesn't draw away. Instead, he whispers, "I want to know all of you."

I don't waste a single moment wrapping my legs around Orlie because I need him again. I want to know all of him too.

8

———

ORLIE

I wake up to a wet kiss against the inside of my thigh. Groggily, I open my eyes and look toward the windows.

These aren't the windows of my room. In fact, this isn't my room at all.

This is Kira's room. I'm still in her bed.

And she's between my legs, a lump beneath the sheets.

"What time is it?" I ask although I don't care much about that when I feel her lips trailing higher and higher toward my half-hard cock.

"Does it matter?"

"No, just –" I'm cut off by her lips wrapping around the head, a long sigh slipping through my lips. "Jesus Christ..."

Kira laughs around me, causing shockwaves of delight through my groin. As her lips slide up and down my length, taking me deeper and deeper, I harden more and more. Hard to believe I can even get hard again when we went three times last night without stopping.

I let my head fall back into the pillow, squinting my eyes

at the sunlight streaming in through the windows. My hips start to rise and fall, trying to follow Kira's lips.

It's good to know she hasn't snuck out of bed, regretful of what happened last night. I'm certainly not.

But...

It does feel like if we're going to do this, there should be some ground rules. Something that keeps us both from getting hurt.

Because I'm her boss. And we have to work together after this.

"Wait, wait, wait..." I begrudgingly interrupt her delicious rhythm.

Kira pops me out of her mouth and lifts the covers to look at me. "You okay?"

I have to take a beat; Kira in the morning takes my breath away. Leaning in between my legs, her breasts hanging down, ruby nipples perked and in desperate need of my mouth. Her hair mussed from sleeping and all the fine work we did together last night. Her glasses up on her head, eyes trying to keep me in focus.

Beautiful. Just beautiful.

"I'm great, I just..." I touch her shoulder and draw her up into my arms. She settles onto my chest with a happy sigh. "We should talk about this."

"About what?" she asks, playing dumb.

I chuckle and tip her glasses down from her head over her eyes. "I'm sorry, were you too drunk to remember all the fucking we did last night?"

Her eyes roll up. "Ohhh...you want to talk about all the fucking we did last night."

Before I can reply, she kisses me. My toes curl. What the hell is Kira Solace doing to me? I knew from that one dance we had together that there was something electric between us. However, I couldn't have possibly anticipated a connection as intense as this. One kiss from her sends my body into overdrive.

I'm terrified I might need her.

That's something I'll have to keep to myself for now, though.

"I think it would be good to talk about it," I say. "Especially seeing as you were already eagerly –"

Kira reaches down and cups my erection. My eyes flutter shut, mouth parting.

"Something to do with this?"

"Christ, I can't think when you –"

She removes her hand and holds it up in the air. "Fine, I'll play fair."

"Thank you." I'm not sure why I'm thanking her for taking her hand *off* my cock when I very much would like her to be all over it. "Anyway, um…"

"Let me guess," she says and then takes a deep breath. "You'd like to continue doing this for the remainder of our time here as long as we can do it objectively without anyone catching feelings. Am I right?"

My eyebrows jump. "Took the words out of my mouth. How'd you know that?"

For a split second, something like disappointment pops onto Kira's face, although I'm not sure that's what it is.

"Just makes sense. Given that we work together."

"Yeah," I say. I'm not able to veil my disappointment either, really.

"And I personally really enjoyed last night, so it'd be silly to stop if we know we're still going to be spending all this time together."

"Exactly."

"And even if there were feelings..." Kira trails off. I stop breathing. "We wouldn't make sense in the long run."

I screw my forehead together. "What do you mean by that?"

A smirk crawls across her face. "Come on, Orlie. We work together."

Yes, obviously. "You already said that."

"Okay, well. It's a good enough reason to mention twice."

I'm about to ask her to clarify even further, but don't have time before her hand slips around my balls. "Now, can I get back to what I was doing?"

The gentle massage of her hand is too good to pass up. "Uh-huh."

Kira smiles. "Thank you."

She disappears under the covers and takes me into her mouth all the way. I go limp into the bedclothes and let her have her way with me, trying to ignore the sinking feeling that there's another reason Kira Solace thinks we would never work.

***

Under the canopy of trees, the temperature is much more tenable, casting me in coolness as I jog down the trail. Hunter wasn't smart enough to install a home gym (or he's just blessed to have a godlike figure due to genetics and the metabolism of a toddler), so I've been forced to do things the old-fashioned way. Bodyweight exercises and jogs.

No matter. I don't need the whole gym experience to keep myself in shape. A trail run first thing in the morning is good for me to clear my head.

Not as good as Kira waking me up with a blowjob, but...

After that first night, we agreed not to sleep in the same bed. That would encourage intimacy. Instead, after a second night of absolute carnal desire, I was forced to walk bowlegged back to the master suite.

However, that means both of us can get a good start to our day so she can work and I can pretend like I'm not working.

Running on the trails is also good because I don't need to wear headphones. I can just enjoy the chirping of birds, the leaves rustling, and the dirt scuffing beneath my feet.

I focus on the bend in the path before me, the curl that leads the trail loop back to the house.

I pick up my pace to a sprint and, once I reach the bend, slow to a stop. I bend over, rest my hands on my knees, and take some deep breaths. Wish I had some water or something to make the jog back a little bit –

"Need a drink?"

I stand up immediately, face to face with Kira. She's wearing a classic running getup. Little shorts, a sports bra, a sweatband to hold her bangs back. She holds out a water bottle toward me.

"Where the hell did you come from?"

"I thought I'd walk to meet you and then we could jog back together."

It's almost creepy if it weren't so incredibly charming and I didn't need this water like my life depended on it.

"Thanks..." I take the bottle of water and chug it as fast as possible.

"Easy there, big boy."

I spill the water over my chin. *Big boy* does something to me. I swipe my hand down my face to clear away the water and the sweat.

"Didn't know you ran."

"Sometimes. I'm not very fast," she says with a shrug and starts to jog backward. "You'll have to take it easy on me."

Kira turns around, brown ponytail bobbing over her shoulders. My eyes fall immediately to her butt, tight and round in her shorts. Damn, I want a handful of that. A smile curls onto my face and I break into a jog after her.

It doesn't take much for me to catch up to her. But I'm not looking to intimidate her with speed. I'm just enjoying a run in the forest with Kira Solace.

"Got good form," I say.

"Th...thanks," she says between measured breaths.

I've been running long enough that a casual chat during a jog isn't too hard. Clearly, Kira has to focus on her breath. That's just fine. I'll let her have it.

We continue to run. Sometimes, I have to lessen my pace so I'm not two steps ahead of her. Damn these long legs (although I wasn't saying that last night when she wanted to climb me like a fucking tree).

There's a new sound added to the scape of the forest. Kira's breath. Measured inhale through her nose, a tight exhale through her lips.

It's making me hard. Her heavy breathing...I've heard it in the night while I'm inside her. It's like some Pavlovian response: Kira breathes heavily, I get hard and want her.

I start to pick up the pace. I need to get home as fast as possible to deal with this.

To my surprise, Kira keeps up. She follows me, a small laugh falls from her lips. "Are we racing?"

"You're on."

We race the last mile back to the house and, nearly tripping up the stairs, I beat her to the back door.

Kira runs the rest of the way to meet me and presses her

hand against the house, bending over and clutching her side. "Good one," she says through heaving breaths.

I can't stand it a second longer. I press her up against the door, not bothering to heed her gasp, and kiss her as hard as I can. Her heart throbs through her chest, sweat dripping from all of her pours.

"Let me shower," she groans between kisses.

"Can't wait. Need you now."

"That's so..."

Disgusting? Gross?

"Hot. Oh my god, that's so fucking hot." Kira throws herself around me and I push open the door, happy to take her on the first flat surface we can find.

"ORLIE?"

I alert from my place on the couch. I've finally relaxed after days of pacing around the cabin, trying to figure out ways I could work that wouldn't be dubbed working. Kira finally made me pick up a book from one of the tall bookshelves. I've been attempting to read Faulkner, which is just as joyless as it sounds. But giving me something to focus on is good for getting me to unwind.

What's been even better is having Kira and our extracurriculars as an outlet.

We've been sleeping together for five days. That's not all we've been doing. We've taken jogs and hikes together. Had meals together. Watched movies together too. It's like a prolonged sleepover where we also get to fuck.

And man is it *ideal*.

Hearing her call out my name is usually a sign for me to come get her and have my way with her.

But the way she says it from the office is different.

"Could you come look at something for me?"

It's not wanting. It's serious. Like the way she sounds at work when she's talking to her team.

I put my book down and pad into the office where Kira is sitting in the desk chair, knees drawn up and hunched over the computer.

I've seen Kira many ways since I met her and even more so since we accidentally ended up at this cabin together.

This way, with her glasses at the end of her nose, her hair tied into a messy bun, and her brow furrowed as she tries to problem-solve might just be my favorite.

"What's up?" I ask, leaning up against the doorframe as casually as I can.

Her eyes flick up to me. "I'm trying to do some preliminary design of the lobby and I'm having trouble figuring out how best to organize the students. Come look."

I circle the desk and lean over her shoulder to look at the screen. Kira is working with a rough mockup of a classroom from the perspective of a teacher.

"I've put the desks on risers so that the teacher can see everyone –"

"Yeah, that's smart."

"But I still feel like for a classroom of twenty, this is too chaotic for a teacher to look at."

I tilt my head to the side. "I see what you mean. This is just a stopping point, though, right? Between activities?"

"Sure. Yes, but this is the space for questions mid-lesson so that they can continue their VR experience without having to remove the headset."

I smile. "How about you just use some sort of question trigger? That way only those with questions will be filtered into the lobby."

"That makes sense. However, doesn't that eliminate the social element for the kids?"

"Kids in VR can't handle a social element."

Kira smiles and leans her head in her hand. "Oh, come on. That's gotta be a part of the fun, right?"

"Teachers already have it hard enough with kids running amok in the real world, let alone the virtual one."

"Well, there'd be caps on what they can do, of course. It's not like a video game where they can run around and punch things."

"Right, but during a lesson, I think kids should be limited to their activity and access to the teacher."

Kira rubs her chin and nods. "I see your point. Maybe we can work at implementing a social part of the program that teachers can opt to use or students can use for experimentation."

I lean on the edge of the desk. "Not a bad idea."

"It would require more work and probably be the most complicated part of the program apart from actually instituting the subject-specific programs, but –"

"No, you're right, I think it's worthwhile."

Kira smiles. "Really?"

"Yeah, I trust your judgment. Just tell me the timeline and we'll make it happen."

She giggles and leans back in her chair. "Orlie Wynters, who knew you were such a softy."

"I'm not a softy."

"Yeah, you are. I should have fucked you ages ago to get my way, huh?"

My jaw drops, frozen in a surprised smile. "Sometimes, the things you say, Kira..."

"I'm kidding, I'm kidding."

"Oh, no, please don't kid. I love it."

Our eyes meet for a moment. Two moments. Three moments. Too long. I rip my gaze away first. It's fun to tease and play, however, the domestic and working elements of this trip sort of cloud my judgment when it comes to her.

It's easy to be around Kira. Easier than I've ever let it be. And that terrifies me.

"Um. Keep up the good work, alright?" I say and push myself up from the desk.

"You got it, boss."

That goes right to my dick; I disappear into the bathroom to deal with that one on my own.

KIRA IS CURLED UP INTO MY CHEST AS A MOVIE PLAYS on the television. I'm not sure what she's chosen to watch. Some romcom with Meg Ryan. I can never tell them apart. Doesn't matter. Anything could be on. As long as I'm here with her, it doesn't matter.

Her hand rests on my belly which is full after a delicious, indulgent meal: salmon, asparagus, garlic whipped potatoes, all complemented by a zingy white wine. I resist the urge to grab her hand and let my fingers tangle with hers.

"I wish I had hair like Meg Ryan," she remarks with a heavy sigh.

I chuckle and push some hair out of her face. "I like your hair just the way it is."

Kira's eyes flutter shut. "You're sweet."

"Just telling the truth."

"Sure." She doesn't open her eyes again.

We could fall asleep like this, sure. But I'm antsy. Not ready to go to bed.

We've had sex every night for a week. I'm almost scared to break the cycle. What if the second we stop, she realizes that we shouldn't be doing this or she changes her mind? I know I would be a total wreck if she cut me off early.

"Kira."

"Hm."

"Wake up."

"Why?" she asks, pushing her face into my chest.

"Let's do something."

"Like what?"

I slink out of her grasp, movie playing in the background. Kira grunts in frustration. "Orlie, where are you going?"

I pull my shirt off, then go in for the pants.

"Orlie! What are you –"

"I'm going for a dip."

Kira pushes her glasses up her nose. "What?"

"In the hot tub," I say. I let my pants drop to the ground and then jerk my head to the back door. "Come on."

I head out onto the back porch. Kira stumbles after me. "What? But your swim trunks are –"

"Don't pretend like you didn't catch me out back when you got here getting out of the hot tub naked," I say with a casual laugh.

Kira crosses her arms over her chest. "It's not sanitary."

"The water is practically boiling. Of course, it's sanitary."

"That's not how that works."

I roll my eyes. Her playful resistance will only last so long before she gives in. "You're being paranoid." I pull my briefs down and then step into the hot water. "Oh, that's nice. Perfect temperature."

"Orlie!"

"What?!" I drop into the tub and sit in the corner, spreading my arms out. "It's nice. Come on in."

Kira frowns. "I'm not getting into the hot tub naked."

"It's not anything I haven't seen before."

"It's not that, it's –" She shakes her head. "I'm not doing it."

Okay, this resistance is clearly not as playful as I'd thought. "Kira, seriously, it's not a big deal. We can cuddle in here."

"Orlie, I don't want to. Alright? The idea of being in the hot tub naked makes me uncomfortable."

I scoff. "You can't be serious."

"I am serious."

"Don't be a bore, Kira. Just come on in and..." I trail off when I see how her expression curdles.

Kira's whole body has tensed in a way I've never seen, her head ducking down almost like a turtle trying to hide in its shell. Her fists tighten at her hips.

"I said *no*. What don't you get about that?"

"I'm –" Shit. I've crossed a line. However, I never thought it would be over skinny dipping in the hot tub. "Okay, you said 'no'. Got it. I was just trying to have a little fun."

"Well, this doesn't seem fun to me."

"Trust me, that much is obvious."

Kira stares at me with laser intensity through her glasses, which only seems to magnify the beams more.

"Kira, listen –"

"I'm going to bed. Goodnight."

Without another word, Kira stomps into the house. I'm left with my mouth ajar, gobsmacked by her outright dismissal of me. After a week of developing whatever this is, she's just going to walk off after a little tiff that she created out of nothing?

Now *my* fists are clenched and I'm furious. How could she do this to me? Walk off without letting me have a second chance.

I should have known this was how it would be from the start. There was no reason to complicate our working relationship. In fact, I should have left immediately when she arrived. Ignored the feeling in my gut I've had all this time since we danced together at Hunter's wedding.

That would have saved us both a lot of trouble.

And it would have saved me some heartache I don't want to acknowledge in my chest.

9

———

KIRA

I fold up the last of my laundry and stick it in my suitcase. Screw a month. A week and change stuck in this cabin with Orlie has been more than enough. I need a vacation from my vacation.

If you can even call this a vacation at all.

Outside, rain patters against the window. A major June storm is rolling in to signify the impending arrival of summer. These are usually my favorite kinds of storms. We never get them in LA unless there's some natural disaster happening.

Now I can't even stay and enjoy it.

I tossed and turned all last night after what happened.

How could he do that to me?

Maybe I should have just gotten into the tub and ignored it. Could have avoided the confrontation altogether if I just gave in.

But that's not who I am. I don't give in to avoid people being upset with me. I didn't want to get into the hot tub naked. What's so crazy about that?

Orlie has seen me in plenty of the rooms of this house naked before. He didn't need me in the tub naked too.

He's gotten greedy.

And I think it's time we end this.

I zip up my suitcase and sigh. This was supposed to be relaxing. I wasn't supposed to be dancing on my every last nerve around my boss, wasn't supposed to be giving into temptations about him, wasn't supposed to be fighting with him.

Home. That's where I need to be.

I grab my bags and head out of my room and down the stairs. I can hear Orlie in the kitchen, the radio on. Who listens to the radio anyway?

I make it through the front hall and out the door before Orlie notices. I hear his footsteps heavy behind me. He says something too, but I don't hear it over the humongous roll of thunder that shakes the house.

I continue down the stairs and into the rain. It's heavier than I thought. I'm drenched by the time I get to the car.

"Kira, stop!" I finally hear Orlie's voice. He grabs my shoulder and flips me around. "Where the hell are you going?"

He followed me out into the rain. That has to count for something, right?

Orlie looks at me with those darker-than-dark eyes, a frown of confusion on his forehead.

"I'm going home." I start to load my bags into the backseat.

"You can't go anywhere in this storm. Are you crazy?"

"I'd be crazy to stay here a second longer."

Orlie stares at me. "You can't be serious."

"This was all a mistake," I say and shrug off his touch, rounding the car to the driver's seat. "I should have turned right back around when we realized there had been some miscommunication between Amy and Hunter and –"

"You're not going out in this storm. Wait until tomorrow at least. I won't stop you, but there's no way I'm –"

"Orlie, I'm a grown woman. I can make my own decisions."

His T-shirt is soaked through, showing off the brilliant curves of his pecs, the bumps of his nipples. Dear god, I'd love to tear it off him.

In another life, maybe.

"Of course you can, but this is insane! Do you know what Hunter would do to me if I let you go out there like –"

"Not my problem," I say with finality and get in the car.

I'm chilled to the bone, but to hell with it. Once I get off this fucking mountain, then I can deal with being cold. I turn on the car, flick on the high beams, and start out of the driveway.

Orlie stands and watches. Totally creepy. I try not to give him one last glance as I head down the long private drive, back to the highway. My heart is already feeling lighter as I leave Orlie in my wake. I'll deal with the fallout once we're both back at work.

If my calculations are correct, there won't *be* any fallout. Orlie and I will go back to the way things have been since... well, since forever. We can ignore what happened between us and just go about our lives. Keep our heads down, do our work and –

I stomp on the brake when I reach the wooden bridge. Because there's no bridge to be seen. If I were to continue driving, my car would tip into a torrent of rushing muddy water that was barely a trickling stream when I arrived.

I clutch my chest and take some breaths. That could

have been bad if I'd let my thoughts spiral any further out of control.

And then it dawns on me...

I have to go back. Unless I want to sleep in my car where I'm frozen to the bone and don't have any food and just wait out this storm for god knows how long.

Which means going back like a puppy with its tail between its legs to Orlie Wynters.

How fucking embarrassing.

I slam the door to signify my arrival. Orlie nonchalantly emerges from the kitchen, running a towel through his hair. "You're back."

"The bridge is out."

"I heard."

I furrow my brow. "And you just let me –"

"It just came on the radio, relax," Orlie says and retreats back into the kitchen.

Through the pound of rain on the roof, I can hear the staticky voice on the radio. "*Stay off the roads, stay away from windows, and get ready for a long couple of days, folks.*"

I pull my suitcase back into the front hall and then curse. It's soaking wet. I don't want to pull it through the house, back to my room.

"Here."

I get a face full of towel a second later.

"Sorry, thought you were ready."

It's dry and warm. As if Orlie has just pulled it out of the dryer for me. "Thanks," I grumble.

"My pleasure."

Yeah, right.

Calm down, Kira...he's being nice. I can't help it that my temper comes out when I'm too cold.

"Get out of those wet clothes and into something dry, huh? I'll make you some tea."

"I don't want any tea."

Orlie sighs. "Fine."

I grab what I need out of my suitcase and retreat to my room, putting on some dry clothes. I still feel chilled to the bone, unable to get warm, especially now that the towel has lost most of its heat.

I go into my bathroom and turn on the hot water. As I wait for the bath to fill up, the lights flicker and the power goes off, leaving me in total darkness.

"*Shit.*"

No power means no furnace. Which means no hot water. Which means –

"FUCK."

"WELL, I COULDN'T FIND THE GENERATOR," ORLIE announces as he climbs up from the basement and back into the living room.

I am bundled in every blanket I could get my hands on, staring into the room. It might be the middle of the day, but this storm makes it seem like it's the dead of night. We have a few candles lit around the room and a lantern with a hand crank Orlie found in the closet.

"You still don't have any signal, right?"

"Right," I say without looking at my phone. The only way we've been able to get in touch with anyone while up here has been on the wi-fi. Which is, of course, down, due to there being no power.

Orlie goes to one of the easy chairs and sighs. "Well. This sucks."

"Tell me about it."

He raises his eyes to me. "Yeah, sorry you're stuck here with me."

"Watch your tone."

"No tone. A genuine apology considering how eager you were to get out of here this morning. Wouldn't want to make you feel crazy for staying."

I close my eyes and lean back on the couch. Yes, I was sort of nasty, wasn't I? "I'm sorry I said that."

"Whatever."

Hard to believe that only twenty-four hours ago, we were still locked in our infatuation for one another. Now, disdain is at an all-time high. "Let's just pretend this isn't happening, alright?" I say.

"Couldn't have said it better myself."

I FALL ASLEEP NOT LONG AFTER THAT. THE WARMTH OF my nest of blankets finally brings my temperature back up and I'm able to feel cozy and safe.

I'm awoken by a large blast of thunder that shakes the windowpanes and a growling in my belly. "What time is it?" I ask through my nest.

"Ah, you're up." Orlie is still in his chair, book in hand. "Mid-afternoon."

I slough off some blankets and go toward the kitchen.

"I made some sandwiches if you're interested. All the meat is going to go bad if the power doesn't kick back on so —"

"Great, thanks," I grumble. I try not to marvel at the

beautiful roast beef sandwiches Orlie has somehow created. And I try even harder not to audibly groan at the first bite. Don't want to give him the satisfaction that I actually might enjoy him or anything he does ever again.

I return to the living room with a plate of chips and the sandwich and enjoy it in silence.

Well, almost silence. Sure, there's the rainstorm outside. But there's also Orlie.

He's focused very intently on the book he's reading. And each time he turns the page, he has to lick his fingers, making an ugly slick sound that grates down my spine.

I try to ignore it, but I just can't. "Do you have to do that?"

Orlie lifts his eyes. His face is as apathetic as it always has been. Until I started catching his smiles. Some part of me still craves one of those smiles, even though I'm one hundred and ten percent done with whatever Orlie and I were for the past week. "Do what?"

"The licking your fingers thing. It's…annoying."

"I need to be able to turn the page."

"Normal people turn the page without licking their fingers."

"When have you ever considered me a normal person, Kira?" The tone of his voice as he asks that question causes a shiver down my spine, this time not from my body temperature. "And besides, you're the one there crunching on chips with your mouth open."

I gape. "I do not chew with my mouth open!"

"You were just a minute ago."

I look down at my half-eaten plate and put it on the coffee table as if it's diseased. "I don't."

"You did."

"Oh my god, you're impossible."

"So I've been told."

"An obvious only child."

He rolls his eyes and returns to his book.

I go grab the radio from the kitchen. It has a hand crank to generate power, good in an emergency such as this. I start to turn the crank, desperate to hear a voice other than Orlie's even if just for a minute.

"What are you doing?"

"Want updates on the storm."

"Newsflash: It's still raining."

I growl, throwing the radio down on the couch, and heading to the window to look out at the property. The acreage is already swamped. We can't take much more of this.

"Kira, stay away from the windows, alright?"

"Don't tell me what to –"

A major flash of lightning followed immediately by thunder sends the windows shaking harder than they have all day. I leap back, letting out a terrified squeal, and land right in Orlie's arms.

He pulls me into his chest for a prolonged moment. My body melts as if nothing happened last night. As if we never got into an argument to begin with. His embrace feels like home.

"I told you, stay away from the windows," he murmurs.

I push him off abruptly. He can't let a nice thing be nice for one fucking second. "I told you, don't tell me what to do."

"I wouldn't have to if you weren't being so difficult," he says and reaches for my wrist to pull me away from the window.

"Don't touch me!"

Orlie raises his hands in the air and glares to the side.

"God, why are you being like this?"

"Like what?"

"Impossible!"

"It's better than boring, isn't it?" I snap.

Orlie takes a step toward me and points to the center of the room. "Get back in the room or so help me god, I'll –"

"What? Make me?!"

Apparently, that was enough to poke the bear. Orlie scoops me up over his shoulder and tosses me down on the couch. "Sit *down*."

"What the hell is wrong with you?!"

"Me?! You've been treating me like I'm some sort of villain since last night. You almost killed yourself out in the rain to get away from me!" he shouts back.

"Because you called me a bore!" I reply.

Orlie goes silent. The pattering of rain intensifies. The corner of his mouth perks up as if I've made some sort of a joke. "That's why you're upset with me?"

My jaw tightens. "Don't smile. It's not funny. It's not some sort of joke."

He shakes his head vehemently. "No, no, I'm not laughing. I'm just confused."

I grip the edge of the sofa and look away.

"I just said it to get under your skin, not to –"

"People think I'm boring and they leave. It's as simple as that."

Rain. Pitter pattering. Me. Wanting to disappear into the couch.

"What do you mean, people think you're boring?" Orlie moves to sit at the edge of the coffee table right across from me.

My heart thumps in my chest. "Just. I'm a nerd. You've said it yourself before. I hide in the background. Not the type to have all eyes on me. Because of that, I've grown to like my space. I like things my way. I don't like to be pressured to be anything I'm not. And skinny dipping in a hot tub is most certainly something I'm not."

"I would never want you to be something you're not."

I lift my eyes to his. There's the Orlie I've grown to adore over the past week. The one that makes my insides melt together into a sticky mess of god knows what.

"A lot of people haven't felt that way. A lot of men have...changed their minds about me. Decided I'm not worth keeping around because I'm..." I lift my hands and then let them drop. "I'm not enough the way I am, I guess. I'm a bore."

"Kira, I just said that word because it was the first thing that came to mind, it wasn't –"

"Words don't just come out of thin air, Orlie. It's nice to think they do, but they don't."

We are both quiet. Orlie reaches out and takes my hand. "Look, I'm sorry what I said hurt you. It was never my intention to make you think I really believed that with my core. This week..." He trails off and then decides against whatever he was thinking of saying. I silently beg for him to go on, but he doesn't. "I know how hard it can be to forget the things an ex has done or said. Believe me."

I'd be foolish to believe Orlie has never been hurt. But where is this coming from? Who hurt him? And what did she do? I wish we were closer so I could ask. In a way that I might even deserve to know.

Orlie touches my cheek. "Kira, come back to me. Please."

The decision to despise Orlie Wynters from last night immediately fades away. I feel myself falling into his arms once again. And I don't resist for a moment.

10

___

ORLIE

I DRAW KIRA INTO MY ARMS AND KISS THE SIDE OF HER head. A small patch of hair is still distantly damp from her early rain shower. Her body feels so small in my arms. I want to protect her. I want to find every man who ever hurt her and give them a piece of my mind.

How could anyone find her boring? She's the most mysterious woman I've ever met and somehow, even more delightful to know. I have yearned for her since the second I saw her, even before our names touched each other's mouths.

And with a careless little word, I let her spend a night hating me. Pushing me away.

"Orlie –"

Before she can speak, I press my lips to hers, turning her words into a longing sigh. "Don't walk away from me again," I whisper. "Please don't."

She hooks her arms around my neck and kisses me harder, nearly knocking me back onto the coffee table. I slide my hands down to her waist, then to her hips, taking handfuls of her curvaceous ass. Heaven.

We fumble onto the ground, clawing at clothes, pulling in directions that will never get them off. We're so desperate we don't even have common sense.

Kira is above me, riding the ridge of my cock through our clothes, her chest pressed to mine, kissing me with primal need. I can't seem to keep up with her.

"Slow down, slow down," I entreat her.

Kira's lips break from mine. She presses her face into my shoulder and stops just long enough that I can cradle her right there to my chest.

"How can you possibly think you're boring?" I ask, voice weaving through her hair.

She shakes her head. "I don't know. I've always been quiet."

I want to tell her that quiet doesn't mean boring. That quiet is what I've liked about her all this time. Not quiet as in docile. Quiet as in determined. Confident. Captivating.

"I'm quiet too, aren't I?" I ask.

"It's different. You're…"

I wait on pins and needles for her explanation.

"People have to look at you. No one has to look at me."

I draw away enough to look into her eyes. "I have to look at you. There's no way I could look away from you."

Her lips perk up.

Say it back. Something back. Anything to let me know I'm not alone in this.

I want nothing more than to follow in my father's footsteps. Be the good CEO I've been trained to be. That definitely doesn't include having sex with my employee. Doesn't include being in a relationship with her either. But I think I want both.

Scratch that, I know I do. We could fucking run Wynters together. We'd be unstoppable.

Kira grabs my cock through my shorts, reminding me that it's not good to think or make decisions while horny. "How do you want me?"

"I..."

Thunder swallows my answer. Or did I not answer at all? All I know is that just a moment later, Kira is over me while my back is propped up against the couch, cock standing tall and erect. She hovers over me, notching me into her entrance, and then sinks down my entire length, her head tipping back with sweet release.

I gasp. "Holy fuck."

"I'm hot," she whispers and then rips off her T-shirt, revealing her bare chest.

I can't resist pulling her chest toward my mouth and wrapping her nipples in my mouth, trading off between the two of them so neither feels unwanted.

"Keep doing that, it feels –" Kira's moan finishes the sentence.

I watch her face as I suck on her tits, not even worried about the spasm building in my core. I brace my feet against the floor, joining in her thrusting while my tongue winds around her perky nipple.

"Faster," she whines.

I don't have enough leverage to do what she wants like this. I fling her off my lap and press her onto the couch. "Want you from behind."

"Yes, do it, do it."

I don't want her to lose her momentum. I slide into her, hooking my hands around her waist, and let out a string of curses. She feels so good. So tight. So welcoming. She hasn't lost that first-time feeling ever since the beginning.

A roll of thunder rocks the house and, as if that's something happening inside Kira's body, she moans. One with nature. A force to be reckoned with.

I run my hand along her jaw, cupping her chin in my hand, and yank her back to whisper in her ear. "Let me know how good I make you feel."

She whimpers.

"Let the world know."

Her pretty ruby lips part. I catch her next moan in my mouth, letting it shake my insides. Suddenly, I'm thrusting at a speed I didn't know possible, sliding in and out at break-neck speed, wishing I could somehow go deeper, let her swallow me whole.

Kira reaches back for me, hand slapping at my side. She finally lands her grip around my ass, digging her fingernails into it. Her grip drives me to pound into her and with each one, I feel the coil inside of her tighten until she rips her mouth from mine and wails.

Lightning clouds my vision, leaving me starry-eyed. I'm not sure if it's the storm or just the orgasm tearing through my body that does it, but whatever it is, I am drenched in ecstasy.

Kira buries her face in the couch cushion, letting out the last of her keens while I've gone mute, face slack with relief of the pent-up pleasure. I needed her last night. Needed her even more now.

I'm not sure I can let her go.

I start to press a line of kisses across her back, nuzzling her, wanting her to know just how special she is to me.

Midway through the row, Kira pushes me away. I have no choice but to withdraw from her, my cock all sad and soft looking, coated in her juices and growing cold.

"We can't keep doing this," she says and reaches for her T-shirt.

I'm not sure I've heard her correctly. "Huh?"

"You're my boss. It – it doesn't make sense."

There goes all my hope. No. Delusion.

She's right. It doesn't make sense and it never will.

But if she's right, why does my whole body ache at her saying it?

"I'm sorry," she says, though it doesn't feel genuine since she's not looking at me. "I think maybe what happened last night might have been a sign that we are...in over our heads."

Every choice I make is calculated and precise. Except for Kira. I could say I saw it coming a mile away, but I didn't. Kira was not in my plans.

That's how it should remain.

I clear my throat. "No, you're right. It was foolish."

Her shoulders jump. "I didn't say that."

I push myself up off the ground and grab my clothes, putting them on as fast as possible. Being naked in front of her feels way too vulnerable right now. "Don't worry about me. I'll pretend as if it never happened."

"Orlie –"

"That's what you want, right?" I ask.

Our eyes meet across the room. Thunder. More distant this time. Kira remains silent for a moment before nodding slowly. "I guess you're right. That's what's best."

I run my hand through my hair. I want to shrivel up and die for even thinking there was a chance something could exist between us. I'm not made for love. That much was clear before we started.

I thought, though, maybe, with Kira, I could have a chance. Maybe I had found the person to try again with. Being a hopeless romantic doesn't look good on me, though.

It's a waste of time and effort. "I need to use the bathroom," I say, and walk away before she can say anything else.

Once the door is shut, I close the toilet, sit down on the lid, and drop my head in my hands.

11

———

KIRA

"Miss? You alright?"

I am roused from some dream I immediately forget about when I notice a strange man standing over me, his hand jostling my shoulder.

"Jesus Christ, who are you?!" I yelp, throwing myself into the corner of the couch. I reach for my glasses, fumbling until I get them twisted in my fingers. The second I throw them on, the world comes back into focus.

The man, an older fellow with a dusty mustache and a baseball cap on his head, holds his hands up. "I'm sorry, I didn't mean to scare you!"

"What are you doing in here?"

"I manage the property for Mr. Ricks. Name's Gerald, Miss."

I remain incredibly still, going so far as to hold my breath. The man looks nice enough. His hands are up in surrender. If he wanted something from me, I'm sure he already would have taken it. And if he broke in, I certainly didn't hear it. I was sound asleep.

I notice for the first time, the house is quiet. No rain. In fact, the sun is streaming in through the skylights.

"Wait, how did you get here? The bridge –"

"Town's already gotten it back in order. Rush job. Couldn't have anyone stranded up here."

I sit up straighter. "And you got in…"

"With a key, Miss." Gerald holds up a ring of keys. "I promise, I'm just here to check on the grounds and make sure the power was back on. Mr. Ricks told me he had some family staying up here and bid me to come check on you. Glad I did, otherwise you might have been stranded out here for a while."

I scan the room. "And the power?"

"Got the generator up and running for you, Miss. Took the liberty of throwing out some of the spoiled groceries."

"Where's…"

"The gentleman you were here with just left."

My heart sinks. "He left?"

"He was the one who got the bridge all sorted out so fast. Privately built, rush job. Not cheap. In fact, once he got the all clear, he was the first to drive across it."

Orlie left. Left me here.

At least he didn't leave me stranded, I'll give him that.

But he left me alone. Maybe I don't deserve to feel broken up about that. I was the one who told him that we had to end things. Maybe this is what I deserve.

I had to do that, though. I couldn't let him break my heart again. Even if he hadn't meant to, even if he apologized. He's my boss. And if I'm going to continue working at Wynters Group without issue, I can't be afraid that he might hurt me.

"I'd be happy to go run some errands for you, Miss, if you like."

"No, no, that won't be necessary." I get up and straighten myself out. I must have fallen asleep pretty early last night. From the looks of the easy chair and the mussed blanket, I bet Orlie slept there. Slept in a room with the woman who'd just told him no.

I shouldn't feel bad. Orlie Wynters probably needs to hear more noes. Growing up with all that money, it probably took him years to know the meaning of the word.

"Thank you for checking on me," I say to Gerald.

"Of course, Miss...?"

"Kira. My name is Kira."

"Happy to help, then."

I smile and skitter out of the room as fast as possible.

He must have left a note, right? Something to say goodbye?

The Wi-Fi is back on. No email or text. Surely, there's something somewhere.

However, after checking the kitchen, his room, my room, every other fucking room, it becomes very clear that Orlie did not leave a note for me. He relied on Gerald to tell me the sad truth.

I've been abandoned in a cabin in the mountains by Orlie Wynters.

This is just rich. Fucking rich. Somehow, after a week of ridiculous bliss together, he's managed to live down to all my expectations. He's cold, heartless, thoughtless, and selfish.

The only reason *I* pulled away was because I knew it was either him or me who would do it first. I wasn't going to let him break my heart. And surely my pulling away didn't break his heart, only shuffled his timeline around.

God forbid someone get in the way of a businessman's timeline.

I know I'm being unreasonable right now, and that I was being difficult, letting him know I wasn't happy around him, but I didn't deserve being left like this. Did I?

After searching for a note that isn't there, I go outside and take a deep breath. Smells amazing out. Everything is green and wet, ready for summer to burst into life.

The only thing bursting from me, though, is a torrent of tears.

I TAKE A DRIVE DOWN THE NEW BRIDGE, WHICH STILL scares the shit out of me. It might not be creaky and wooden, but it was built in a matter of, what, hours? That doesn't seem reasonable. My head is spinning.

I could go back home, take the long drive, forgo the vacation altogether.

Or I could do what I came here to do. Work and be alone.

Orlie being here was a fluke. He wasn't supposed to get in the way. I have three more weeks to fix all this and I intend to use them.

I go back to the roadside store, pick up more food and ingredients, no longer relying on three-course meals every night cooked by Orlie Fucking Wynters. I let myself have this second chance.

I will treat this last week with Orlie as some sort of fever dream. I will never think of it or speak of it ever again if I can help it. And I can.

I'm Kira fucking Solace, dammit. I'm the star employee of Wynters Group. And nothing is going to interfere with that. Not even a fever dream.

12

———

ORLIE

There's a knock on my office door. I lift my head and smile at my confused father. "Hey, Dad."

"What are you doing here? I thought you were taking a vacation. A long one."

I shake my head. "Had enough. Wanted to get back to the business."

Dad looks at me dumbfounded while I get up and fetch some documents from my office printer. Things I need for my impromptu presentations to our executives about the direction I want to take over the next ten years.

"You've rarely taken vacations during your tenure as CEO. Why should I set that precedent?" I say, shuffling the documents through my hands.

"Oh, Orlie, I don't want that life for you. Things are changing, you know?"

I laugh. "Have you gone soft? What happened to the dusk 'til dawn grind of Trevor Wynters?"

Dad doesn't look as humored. In fact, there is a sadness in his eyes, corners slightly fallen. "Please tell me you're not trying to become me."

I pause for a moment. "Of course, that's what I'm trying to do."

Dad looks away. "That's what I was afraid of."

"What's the whole point of handing the company over to me if you don't want me to continue running it the way you have?"

My father takes a deep breath. "This is why it's good if I stay on."

I blink and shake my head. "What? Why?"

"Because I've made mistakes, Orlie. I made a lot trying to dedicate my life to this company. I missed out on so much. And I've always been afraid that you might miss out on your own life too."

I stare at my father. There is a tremoring fear behind his eyes I can't just wish away or ignore.

"You're being dramatic, Dad," I say with a light chuckle, though there's nothing to laugh at. "This is what I went to school for. I was literally born to do it." I cross the room and pat him on the chest. "You've got nothing to worry about, I promise."

I'm clearly not convincing. But he doesn't say another word. Thank goodness for that. Instead, he follows behind me quietly as we head to the conference room. My brain is buzzing. Not with thoughts of my presentation, but with questions about what my father just said.

How can he say all of that to me when I've spent my whole life admiring him and working to be like him for the exact purpose of filling his shoes one day?

More than ever, I'm livid over how he's keeping me from my birthright. The very thing I've been told I'd do since I was a child. If he didn't want me to be like him, he should have acted differently. Or not loved me. Or something, anything that could have changed my trajectory.

Now, it's too late. I'm a machine. I clock in at work and I do my best to make this company better than it was before.

It's what I've always wanted to do.

In the back of my mind, though, is a beautiful brunette I wish would disappear. Kira and her big brown eyes magnified by the lenses of her glasses.

It truly pained me to leave her at the cabin. I just didn't see another way, though. I could stay there and suffer, waiting for her to wake up and see me again the way I thought she did. Or I could throw myself back into work and forget.

Joke's on me, though. There's no way I can forget her after everything we did together. After how close we became.

I don't know how she was able to throw that all away like she did.

If anything, her rebuff proved to me further that I'm made for one thing and one thing only. And that's to be the CEO of Wynters Group.

My father will have to see that. He just has to.

"Over the next three years, I'd like to expand the education sector," I explain, the light of the projector beaming into my eyes. "After our project with Leon Prep, we'll be at the forefront of some big advancements regarding STEM in our school systems. The faster we go, the harder we do it, the more accessible it can become."

I hear a cough among the executives. Accessibility has never been one of their foremost concerns. But it is mine.

"With the parasocial relationship our consumers have with corporations, it's imperative we try and make

Wynters likable and worth supporting, especially to Gen Z."

A quiet grumble. These guys hate Gen Z.

"Who would be helming this project, Orlie?" my dad asks.

My mouth grows dry. "Kira, of course." Just saying her name sends rockets through my bloodstream, right to my crotch. How can a four-letter name wreck me like that?

"Kira needs to be on our top projects," my father says, tightening his arms over his chest.

"This is *going* to be one of our top projects."

He glances at the executives beside him. "I mean, money-making projects."

"If we can develop programming that ends up at the university level, we can get involved with state-funded institutions. Those would be huge contracts."

My dad scratches his chin. "You have a point, but...once Kira is finished on the Leon Prep project, I need her back in the social application pool."

I can't believe he's undermining me like this.

Well, actually, I can. And that's what makes it sting.

"Can I get back to my plan, please?"

***

I somehow make it through the rest of the presentation without losing my grip on reality. But the second I can get out of that conference room, I bolt, rushing right into the bathroom. I've had half an erection since I mentioned Kira's name.

"Fucking shit," I mutter, releasing myself into my hand. My head dips back as I stroke myself with a vicious speed. I come in less than a minute right into the toilet bowl.

What a fucking embarrassment.

I lean my head up against the cool metal of the bathroom stall and sigh heavily. I'm trying too hard to be the man I've always been told I'd become. To be CEO Orlie Wynters. Not son of the CEO. I've given up everything to become this. And that's still not enough.

Furthermore, my mind is still stuck on a woman in a cabin in the mountains. A woman who rejected me and made it clear that because of my role, my title, she couldn't be mine.

What does that title even mean if no one will give it to me?

I'm never going to be enough for anyone, am I?

13

KIRA

Three weeks in the mountains, Orlie-free, turned out to be exactly what I needed to get the Leon Prep project all in order. Now, back in California, my first order of business is family. Always is.

And today's project is Amy's book launch.

Her latest book in her Petunia the Porcupine series is one about Petunia's father getting remarried which I believe is an homage to our father's obvious growing attraction toward Victoria Neville, international supermodel who also happens to be his best friend's little sister. He's of course too bashful and dopey to see that she's infatuated with him as well. If they ever ended up together, it would certainly be an opposites-attract love story.

My sisters and I are all rooting for it to happen.

"Eeeep! I'm so glad you're here!" Amy exclaims when I meet her at the signing table.

"Of course. Just tell me what you need."

Fiona, Amy's right-hand woman when it comes to all things books, pats the seat next to Amy. "You're on book-passing duty."

I look at the pile of hardcovered children's books beside the table. It climbs to an absurd height. Based on the line waiting for Amy's signatures, though, I'm not sure it will be enough.

"Okay...welp. Here goes nothing." I take a seat and hand Amy the first book.

Amy grins at the first mother and child in front of the table. "What's your name, friend?"

"Taylor," the little girl smiles.

"Ooh, what a pretty name. I'm Amy." Amy opens the book and scribbles the name and her signature with a big heart. "Thanks for coming to see me today, Taylor. I hope you like my new book."

Taylor takes the book from Amy with a big grin and the mother thanks us both.

"Jeez, you know how to work a crowd," I murmur in her ear.

"Please, I'm just getting started."

I'm not sure how Amy manages to remain so cheerful and peppy as each book crosses the table in front of her. It's clear this is what my sister was born to do. Write children's books and talk to children. Every now and then, she wriggles her left hand and looks down at the engagement ring, now accompanied by a wedding band. At one point, she looks over at me. "So weird doing this with these on."

I resist rolling my eyes. I know she's not rubbing it in. She's my sister and I'm happy for her, more than I can even describe. However, after everything with Orlie, I'm even more embittered by the idea of love than I was before.

To be clear, what Orlie and I had wasn't even close to love. It was sex. Lots of it. Intense and incredible. Not love.

I didn't dare let it get that far.

And it was for the best. Orlie clearly proved what type of man he was by abandoning me at the cabin.

Although, can I really blame him for that? I was the one who rejected him after all, wasn't I?

God...

"Ehem. Book please."

"Sorry," I mutter, sliding another book toward my sister.

To my surprise, the stack of books was indeed enough to get everyone in line their copy. Once the last child has left, skipping off with their copy of *Petunia and the Wedding Party*, Amy lets out a large sigh and leans back in her chair.

"Damn, I don't know how you do it," I mutter.

Fiona smiles and ruffles Amy's hair. "She's a professional, that's how."

Amy waves Fiona off and sighs. "I need coffee. And a pastry."

"Gilly's is right nearby, isn't it?"

Amy smiles. "Perfect. Then you can tell me all about your trip and your time with Orlie."

My face goes red. "Amy..."

"Don't think we're just going to gloss over it and pretend like it didn't happen. Especially after the argument Hunter and I had over the matter."

"Was it really that bad?"

"A lover's quarrel. Besides, the make-up sex was worth it," Amy says with a devilish grin.

My eyes bug out. "Amy, there are children nearby."

"Oh, relax, they can't hear me. Besides, since when did your ears burn over stuff like that?"

Since Orlie Wynters was inside me. "Amy, nothing happened with me and Orlie. We barely talked."

"Uh-huh. Likely story."

"Amy..." I say warningly.

She caps her sharpie and wiggles her fingers, knuckles cracking. "Just tell me what happened."

"Nothing happened. And that's the last I'll say on the subject. Got it?"

Evidently, my words come out much more aggressive than I intended. Amy's eyebrows jump and her eyes crinkle at the corners. The signature, "Ouch," move from Amy.

"Sorry, that wasn't supposed to be –"

"I won't say another word about it, then," she says and whisks off in the direction of the door.

That's not the usual Amy way. Amy usually likes to niggle until you break down and tell her exactly what she wants to hear. She's changed since being with Hunter. For the better in most ways, of course. And even more since becoming a mother to Jessica, the adoption papers having been signed just days after the wedding. Maybe she's practicing not forcing things as much.

There's a small part of me that wishes she had broken me down enough that I would be forced to tell her. Then I wouldn't have to sit on this burning secret a second longer.

"Come on! Gilly's closes in half an hour!" Amy cries out over her shoulder.

I sigh. Orlie's in the past in every way. That's what I promised myself. And I'm not breaking a promise to myself.

Gillian welcomes me with open arms and a tight hug, rocking me back and forth. "Too tight!" I squeak when I finally run out of breath.

My sister pulls back and smiles. "I've missed you!"

You would think I was lost on a deserted island for years

by that reception. "You cut your hair!" I say, touching the ends of her blonde waves.

Gillian flushes. "Just a trim."

"Nothing ever gets past Kira," Amy says, already taking a seat at one of the café tables where Gillian has set up a spread of coffee and various vegan baked goods.

"Welcome home, Kira!" Lola calls out from behind the counter.

"Thanks, Lola," I reply with a wave to Gillian's best friend, now sister-in-law.

"Come sit, come sit. I need you to try out our new recipe."

The new recipe turns out to be vegan maple scones and they're *delicious*.

"So, how was the trip?" Gillian asks.

I feel Amy glance at me from the corner of her eye.

"I heard you ended up there with a...shall we say old friend? One you may or may not have gotten pretty close to at Amy's –"

"She doesn't want to talk about it," Amy intercedes for which I'm both grateful and disappointed.

Gillian's eyes widen. Our younger sister isn't usually so firm. The confusion is enough to send the conversation on a different trajectory.

"I'm still processing everything. I did a lot of good work up there but I just want to cool off before I head back to the office and think about work. You know? Anyway, how are things here?" I take a huge bite of scone so I can't answer any question that might come my way.

Gillian glances around the bakery. "Well, now that the playground is finally done, after the grand opening on Halloween, Axel can focus on other projects. We're talking about expanding."

"Mm!" I say with a mouthful. I hadn't realized the park was so close to being open for business. I'll have to drive past later.

"Yes, exciting. A second location maybe down in Santa Monica or –"

"Axel is thinking Orange County would be good as far as property value goes," Amy explains.

Gillian's face immediately sours. "It's too far."

"Depending on traffic."

I swallow the dry scone and quickly sip my water to get to my question. "Hasn't that always been the goal? First Orange County then San Diego then –"

"To be clear, my goal was to survive owning a bakery and being a single mom," Gillian laughs. "Now that Axel and I are married, there are certainly more options but..." She shrugs. "I'm more focused on family things."

"Like what? Getting Dad married off?" I say.

Amy sticks her elbow in my ribs and I laugh.

"No, no. More like *my* family."

I take another sad bite of scone. Tastes less delicious by the moment and it's not because it's vegan.

My family. Like Gillian has something to claim that doesn't involve us. Or should I say, doesn't involve me. All my sisters have a family that doesn't involve me.

"She's talking about babies, Kira," Amy clarifies.

"Great, got it," I say.

"Don't say that like *you're* not also constantly talking about babies," Gillian teases.

"I never said I wasn't!"

I'm feeling a little faint at the thought of my sisters all openly gabbing not just about their children but procreating. It triggers that green-eyed monster in me. Even though I've always said I'd wait until I was in my thirties, late thirties if I can help it, I can't help but feel like I'm sticking out like a sore thumb in the Solace family.

"Wouldn't it be great, Gilly, if we both got pregnant around the same time and they could be –"

"Stop, that would be so cute," Gillian says, clapping her hands to her face.

I glance over at Lola who looks at me sympathetically. At least someone understands me.

Amy pulls out her phone and starts to navigate toward her menstrual tracking app. "Okay, well, I'm sure our cycles are pretty much synced, so –"

"You're not seriously considering organizing your pregnancies, are you?" I say.

"What's wrong with that?" Amy asks, totally affronted by my question.

Gilly laughs. "I think Kira's right. We don't have to get too technical about it. But you must admit, Kiki, it'd be cute, right?"

I look between my sisters, imagining little versions of them running around, holding hands, being the best of friends.

The jealousy. It boils inside me. "Really cute," I say with a forced smile.

I decide not to say another word on the subject, let them gab and giggle at the idea of their joint baby showers and maternity shoots. It's all great in theory. But pregnancy and children aren't just fun times to be had and not worry about anything else. Those things should be planned and calculated. Life has to totally stop for a thing like that.

I swallow down the rest of my scone.

For the first time, I think I wouldn't mind if my life stopped for something bigger than me. Not the Leon Prep project, but something I could dedicate my life to.

Shaking off the thought, I reach for another scone.

My life doesn't suit that. Besides, I don't have a man to share it with. That's step one of any sort of plan in having a baby, isn't it?

Orlie pops into my mind. I bat the thought away repeatedly.

Even if things made sense between us, he's gotten his tubes tied. And that's as clear a message as any.

Orlie Wynters will never be my future.

14

ORLIE

I DROP THE BOX OF BAGELS ON THE CENTRAL TABLE OF the HR office and then the vat of coffee. I've been making my rounds this week to every department, providing them with some morning treats just because. I'm not sure what compelled me. Maybe it was an effort of distraction. Focus on projecting all this pent-up energy outward, somewhere good.

And I have to say, the thanks I've gotten has made it that much more worth it.

"What's all this?" Meghna, the head of HR, comes over, dipping her head down and scanning the table as if she's never seen a box of bagels in her life.

"It's hump day. Thought you all could use a pick me up."

She smiles at me. "What do you need, then?"

I frown. "What do you mean?"

"Treats only come around when someone needs something." Meghna folds her arms over her chest and taps her acrylic nails on the inside of her arm. "So?"

"Um..." I've never been one to ply people with favors or

treats. It's always seemed disingenuous to me. However, that's my father's oldest trick. Send flowers, a fruit basket, a bottle of champagne, anything to get what you need. Me? I'm just...being nice.

Never thought I'd be that guy, yet here I am.

"Just because? Is that enough of a reason?" I say with a raised eyebrow.

Meghna narrows her eyes. "Likely story."

"...Solace back in today."

I whip around faster than I'd like to at the utterance of Kira's last name. Two members of the department are chatting quietly in a cubicle. "Sorry, did you say something about...Kira Solace?"

The mousey-looking man nods. "Yeah, she's back in from her vacation today."

My heart starts to beat at an absurd rate. "Oh, that's good to know." *Great* to know. I pour a cup of coffee, trying to ignore my shaking hand and then grab a bagel. "Well, enjoy. I'm going to go check on – yeah."

"See, I told you, they always want something," Meghna says with a laugh.

I rush out of the office and toward the elevator. My feet are moving without my permission. My brain has lost control and my heart is in charge.

The past few weeks have been plagued with me trying to push Kira from my mind. She clouds the corners of everything I do. I've tried to forget, tried to move on. But I just can't.

I don't know what I'm going to say when I get down there. I only know I need to see her. I need to see how it feels to be in a room with her again. *If* I can even be in a room with her again without totally losing my mind.

I press the button for the basement and the high-speed

elevator drops down the shaft, dinging open after only a few seconds. I could have used a longer time to meditate on this question, but here I am. The IT floor.

Again, without my brain considering the downsides of what I'm about to do, I navigate directly to Kira's office where she's barely just settled into her desk chair before I waltz in. "Kira!"

"Ah!" she shouts.

"Sorry!"

Kira shakes her head, resetting. "I wasn't expecting you."

"Well. Here I am."

We stare at each other.

"Brought you coffee," I say and place it at the edge of her desk. "And a bagel."

Kira eyes both items carefully. "Oh. Thank you. I didn't know this was part of the 'welcome back' package."

I laugh. Too hard. "That's funny."

Kira doesn't even crack a smile. "How can I help you, Orlie?"

Any hope I had of perhaps amending things back to the way they were is quickly dashed. Now I have to focus on maintaining. Where do we go from here when we know some of the most intimate parts of each other? And yet are committed to being strangers. "I heard you were back. So, welcome back."

"Thank you."

"How was the rest of your vacation?"

She shifts uncomfortably in her chair. "Good."

"Good?"

"Yes."

"Good."

This is going about as poorly as it could, save her forcing

me to leave the room or spitting in my face. "Listen, I'm..." I draw a bit closer, glancing over my shoulder to make sure no one might be lingering in the hallway. "I'm sorry for how we left things. I was..."

"It was a mistake. We both knew that."

Ouch. "Right. Well, that didn't give me the right to act childish and not let you know I was going to leave. So, I apologize for that."

Kira raises her eyebrows and then leans back in her chair. "Thank you."

I clear my throat. My perfectly tailored suit suddenly feels way too tight. I undo the front button and take a deep breath. "Is it hot down here?"

"It's always hot down here."

"Really?"

Kira nods.

"Doesn't heat rise?"

She blinks.

"I'll have to get that checked out."

"Orlie –"

"Before you ask me to leave –" I say, urgently throwing my hand out to stop her. "I want to clarify some things, alright? First and foremost, I don't think you're boring."

"You already said that."

Her lips perk for only a moment, but it's enough to keep me going.

"Yes, well, it bears repeating. Furthermore, you're incredibly important to Wynters Group and I want to make sure that you know that. Both professionally and –" My mouth gets dry. "Personally."

Kira nods. "Thank you."

I lower my voice. "And while what happened between us might have been out of the purview of professionalism, I don't want that to impact how we move forward working together. If we can put our differences aside and continue to collaborate, I think we will be able to accomplish amazing things."

Something tugs at my heartstring saying this. The entire time Kira's been gone, I've been lamenting how she rebuffed me and how I left with a broken heart. I've been turning over the idea of making amends. Face to face with her, though, that's been made clear that not only is she not interested in such a thing, but it was a foolish thought to begin with.

I'll move on.

However, I need to know that we can still remain loyal to one another. Professionally, that is.

"I hope I've made it clear that my work at Wynters is extremely valuable to me and I wouldn't want to jeopardize my position for any reason whatsoever," Kira says, eyes firmly in mine.

"Of course."

"Your father was incredibly generous to take a chance on me."

"It wasn't a chance. Chance involves risk and there's never been anything risky about having you on our team."

Kira smiles.

I hold my hand out. "Truce, then?"

She takes my hand; I regret having initiated a handshake. My body feels so weak at her touch. I remember what it felt like to have her mouth all over me. Her hands. Her words in my ear. The way her pretty pink lips wrapped around the 'o' of my name.

I shake her hand firmly, then withdraw mine as quickly as possible, wiping off the sweat that accumulated in my palm. "Wonderful. Thank you, Kira."

I turn on my heel and start to leave.

"Thank you again for the coffee and the bagel. Cinnamon raisin are my favorite."

I smile sheepishly over my shoulder before darting down the hallway. Fuck if I knew the kind of bagel I grabbed. Now it's some happy accident that I grabbed the exact one she likes.

No, not happy. Nothing happy about that accident.

Just an accident. Like everything between us.

15

———

KIRA

I HAVE NO APPETITE FOR THE BAGEL OR COFFEE ORLIE brought me.

The real welcome back would have been Orlie fucking me on my desk.

I had prepared so hard for this moment. The moment I'd see him again for the first time. I meditated over it, reminding myself he's just a person, just a man. There are so many other men out there. Men that aren't my boss.

And what happens the first second I see him?

I get wet.

Seriously, I feel like I need to change my panties. Thank god I keep an extra pair in my desk drawer.

I couldn't help it. He looked so handsome in his black suit. The way his fingers formed around the button when he unclasped the jacket reminded me of all the times he'd had my center pinched between his fingers, making sure I came and came and came some more.

I've barely been back fifteen minutes and all the work I'd done to curb this appetite I still have for Orlie has gone to shit.

Deep breaths, Kira. I take a few, closing my eyes.

Just a man...a normal man...

That couldn't be further from the truth, though. Orlie Wynters is far from a normal man. He's a perfect specimen with his perfectly sharpened jaw, his high cheekbones, the deep pools of his brown eyes. Not to mention his broad chest, the way he towers over me, how his arms fit perfectly around me.

A truly perverted part of me wishes that the whole interaction had gone a lot differently.

What if he'd come in, slammed the door behind him, and just *taken me?* Pulled me up out of my chair, forced his lips on mine, and demanded my body of me.

I would have been more than willing to give it to him. Swipe everything off the desk and let it become the stage for our dance of depravity. Fuck all the expensive equipment and the hot coffee, let it all tumble to the floor so he could make a mess of me.

He could rip open my stupid blouse, make the buttons pop in all directions. I wouldn't mind as long as his lips landed right against the front of my neck and traveled down to my breasts, the ones he'd enjoyed so thoroughly at the cabin.

Brute strength. That's what I want again from Orlie.

The way he handled me; grabbed me, contorted me, twisted me around. That dark power he has right under the surface that always made him just seem like an asshole was actually just a primal power brewing.

Now that I know, I can't forget about it.

And the only thing better than a bagel and a coffee as a welcome back would have been a good fucking. Plain and simple.

"You good, Kira?"

I snap out of my fantasy to find Polly in the doorway, holding her clipboard with my task list all ready to go. "Wha – yeah! Hey! How are you?" I leap out of my chair to give her a hug.

"Hello, dear, I'm well, how are..." She trails off. "You're all flushed."

"Am I?"

Obviously. Your heart is beating like you're running a marathon.

"Goodness, are you feeling alright?" Polly places the back of her hand to my forehead and then each of my cheeks. "You're sweating!"

I jerk away from her and clutch my hips, laughing maniacally. "Just scalding hot coffee! Ha! Need to –" I grab the bagel and shove a piece in my mouth. "Gotta cool down," I grunt with a mouthful. Not to mention need the carbs. Mm...carbs.

"Oh, are we the lucky recipients of Orlie's goodies today?!" Polly asks with a bright smile.

I force myself to swallow the rest of the bagel. It hurts going down my throat. "What?"

"Orlie's been bringing treats to each department in the mornings this week."

"That's nice of him." It really is. He's never been the type of boss to do anything just because. "I don't know, though. He brought me these himself."

Polly's head jerks back. "He hand-delivered you a bagel and a coffee?"

"Yeah, to welcome me back. I guess."

Her eyes narrow. "That's awfully friendly."

"Yeah, well –"

Polly has no reason to suspect anything between Orlie and me and I intend to keep it that way.

"I think they're worried I'm going to get poached by another company or something."

"You wouldn't leave, would you?" Her slight panic is obvious in her voice and I feel immediately bad.

"No, of course not. Wynters is home."

"Good. I don't know what I'd do here without you."

Polly places my to-do list on my desk and, as she does so, the air conditioning kicks into high gear. A cool blast of air thrums through the room.

"Holy cow, is that the…"

"Orlie said he'd take a look at it, but I didn't think he was actually serious."

Polly shakes her head. "This is unprecedented."

"That our boss is acting like a boss?" I say with a light chuckle, ripping off another piece of bagel.

"No, no. Well, maybe." Her lips twist to the side. "Something's gotten into him. I'm not sure what. But whatever it is, it's good for all of us."

I smile. It's good to hear he's been doing well. I'd worried I hurt him pretty badly up at the cabin.

"He must be in love or something," Polly adds in an excited whisper.

My eyes widen. "What?! What would make you say that?!"

"Everyone's always nicer when they fall in love. That honeymoon phase where you're dancing on air and nothing matters except for all the love you have in your heart. If I didn't know better, I'd say Orlie Wynters has an object of his affection."

Could that be true? Has he found someone else in these three weeks? God, I think I'll die if he has. But when I really think about it, one question keeps popping up over and over. It couldn't possibly be me, could it?

THE MORE DAYS I'M BACK IN THE OFFICE, I'M STARTING to wonder if Polly might be right.

Orlie is...smiling. When I see him in the hall, he doesn't duck his head down and mutter a hello. Instead, he stands tall and smiles winningly. "Hi, Kira. How are you doing?"

How am *I doing?* Orlie never used to ask questions like that. He'd ask, "How's the project coming?" or "Can we move up the deadline on your latest deliverable?"

He never seemed to care about how I actually was a person.

The horrible thing about this is, despite our pledge of professionalism, my heart jumps into my throat every time I see him and I can't seem to formulate a full sentence.

"Good," I try to gulp out every time.

"Good. Let me know if you need anything," is always his godforsaken response.

Who is this man and what has he done with the grumpy, crotchety, bottom-line-driven Orlie Wynters?

My mind keeps playing through what Polly said. *Everyone's always nicer when they fall in love.*

In the three weeks I was gone, did Orlie Wynters meet the love of his life? Is he a totally different person because of her? My heart never fails to crack at the thought. Because against every logical bone in my body, I want it to be me. *I want to be the reason he's changing.*

Kira, you know you can't change people.

Does it count, though, if I didn't even know I was doing the changing?

I've taken to avoiding Orlie as best I can. Which isn't too hard, since our office is in the basement and all I have to do is close my door to get the privacy I need.

Still, though. I yearn for him. In so many ways. My body, my mind…

The only time I leave my little cove is to use the bathroom. Or, if I haven't brought my lunch from home, to go to the cafeteria.

And today just happens to be one of those days.

I fly through the state-of-the-art kitchen at top speed, ignoring the custom risotto station and freshly made rolls of sushi, opting for some simple comfort food: mac and cheese and cornbread. Once I've scanned my badge, I tuck myself onto a stool at the tables facing the window. Always a good option when I don't want to be disturbed. I could of course squirrel my lunch back down to the basement, but the kitchen has a beautiful view of the beach.

Always helps me take a breath. Remember why I'm here.

This will all blow over. Orlie will become so busy we barely see each other and maybe I'll meet someone new. Maybe I should download a dating app to really get my mind off things or –

A plate lands carefully on the edge of my trail. I eye it. A delectable, golden orange piece of peach cobbler with perfectly browned crust. None of that matters, though, compared to the hand gripping the edge of the plate.

I hate that I know his hand so well. It's been all over me. *Inside* me. How could I not?

I follow Orlie's hand up to his arm, up higher and higher until my eyes land in his.

He's smiling at me. Like a genuine smile. And it's adorable.

"What's this for?" I ask.

"Kitchen has outdone themselves today with this. Wanted you to try it. They used grandmother's recipe."

I try not to swoon. He thought of me.

"There's ice cream too, but I didn't want to rush you. I can get you a scoop, though. Vanilla, of course."

"No, this is just fine the way it is, thank you," I say. Even though the peach cobbler looks divine, I'm not sure I can stomach it. I bet it's incredibly sweet. And each bite would be made all the sweeter knowing who gave it to me. Might make me sick.

"You're welcome," Orlie says with a tight nod.

I shift back and forth on my stool and glance over my shoulder. It feels like everyone is staring even though no one is. I'm just paranoid.

"How are things?"

"Things are good."

"Good. Good. Um. I'll leave you to your lunch, then."

I pick up my fork and dig it into the mac and cheese. "Yeah, thanks."

Orlie steps away; the very second he leaves my ether, I want to grab him and pull him back. But I can't.

As he walks through the cafeteria, he's met with greetings from other employees. He says hello to all of them with gusto, gives someone a hearty high five, exchanges banter about Formula One with someone, and he laughs.

Laughs! Loud, with abandon. Uncaring who might hear.

I don't think I can eat another bite. My stomach is in knots.

How am I going to forget Orlie Wynters? Because every part of my body wants to remember.

16

ORLIE

"If anyone has any questions, you can see me or…" I clear the frog out of my throat and glance at my dad. "Trevor. We would be happy to provide you with a more detailed timeline of the next half of this quarter and our hopes for what we can achieve by mid-September."

I close my portfolio and step away from the podium. The conference hall is filled with all the employees of Wynters Group. It's our top-of-the-month check-in and, as this is the first Monday in August, a prime day to make sure we're all on the same page for this quarter.

Dad still insists on being around for every meeting even though behind closed doors we've had conversation upon conversation to try and work out the kinks in our sharing CEO responsibilities. Regardless, I have to maintain a calm face for the company.

As I wade through my employees, who are beginning to get up and return to their workdays, I can't help but let my eyes drift to the back of the room where the tech department usually stands. I get a glimpse of Kira who is chatting with her assistant. Her eyes flick up to me for such a brief moment it feels like it could be an accident.

The past two weeks have been torture. I've done my best to be just her boss. But I can't help reaching out, wishing she'd cross the line before I do so we can fall into each other's arms again.

I've never been like this.

I have always held my career above everything else. I'd never do anything to jeopardize that.

But I think about Kira Solace more than I think about work. I care more about her than I do about work.

Maybe my dad was right. Maybe I'm not ready to be the CEO after all.

I slow my pace and consider walking over before Kira bids her assistant goodbye and walks in the opposite direction of the traffic flow. I frown as she disappears through the service door to the back hallway, rather than joining everyone else to go toward the elevators.

Without second-guessing myself, I spin on my heels and follow Kira's trajectory through the conference hall and out to the back hallway.

While everything at Wynters is shiny, new, and trendy, the back hallway is like any back hallway. A way for all the less shiny, less new things to get around. Back here is where the maintenance office is, where you can access the trash and laundry rooms, and whatever other things are required to make a business like ours run without a hitch.

What could Kira be doing back here?

My mind leaps to the ends of the earth. What if she's dating the kitchen manager? They're always friendly and I've seen him sneak her extra helpings of things before. I thought for sure he was gay, but –

Breathe, Orlie.

This isn't like me. Coming up with ridiculous, unproven stories just to – what – upset me? Keep me grounded.

I spot Kira at the end of the hallway waiting at the service elevator.

Of course she'd take the back elevator. She wants to stay out of the fray. That's classic Kira.

With all the casualness I can muster (which isn't a lot, considering how un-casual I feel about her), I walk toward Kira and the service elevator.

She alerts once I'm about halfway down the hallway, her head snapping toward me. "Hey."

"Hey," I reply. I tuck my hands in my pockets and lean up against the wall opposite her. "Looks like we had the same idea."

Kira's mouth quirks to the side in a smile. "Nobody ever takes the service elevator."

"Yeah, because most people don't mind waiting for the main elevator so they can delay getting back to work," I chuckle. "Not you, though."

She flushes. "These meetings interrupt –"

"Your flow. Sorry about that."

"It's okay. I know they're necessary."

I swallow, letting my eyes fall along the line of her body. She's wearing a cute skirt with an overall top, orange with white daisies patterned all over it, a tiny white tee underneath. I don't know if I've ever seen her in a skirt, actually. Other than the day of Hunter and Amy's wedding.

It's an innocent-looking outfit. Which makes me half-hard without Kira even trying. I know how naughty she can be. She can't hide her true nature in these charming little outfits. I've had her in positions most people would blush at.

Shit. I'm staring at her. I tear my eyes away and adjust my suit jacket with a deep cough.

"Are you alright?"

"I'm fine."

The service elevator doors part, growling loudly. We step inside the mammoth-sized elevator and land beside one another. Barely a few inches apart.

"I hope you don't mind going down first..." Kira says, pressing the B button for basement.

Dear god, of course I don't mind going down. "Not a problem."

The elevator groans. The problem with it compared to the front elevators is that it's slow. However, it's not a problem right now. Not at all.

To be in Kira Solace's orbit for a few extra seconds is everything to me. *Everything.*

"You're awfully quiet," Kira says.

I shoot her a look. "Aren't I usually?"

"You used to be. But lately..." She looks up at me, her lips curved in a smirk. "No."

My abs tighten to prevent my dick from springing completely to life. "What would you like me to say?"

She shrugs. "I don't know. You could say something about my outfit since you've been staring at it."

I laugh despite myself. I didn't know Kira could be so bold. I love it. "Um, well, it looks very nice."

"Thank you."

"Although I can't say it's the outfit I've been staring at." The way I'm acting is completely opposite everything Kira and I discussed two weeks ago. Just friends. Colleagues. Nothing more.

However, she's egging me on bit by bit. And given how tight the crotch of my pants is becoming, I'm not sure I can resist.

Kira opens her mouth to respond. The doors open at the

basement level. She takes a step forward. Disappointment springs through my chest. Until her hand darts to the fifth-floor button and the doors slide shut. "I don't think we're done with this conversation."

I can't hold back. Something in the air. Thick. Hot. Tension pulling me from every angle. The second the elevator starts moving, I grab Kira's arm and push her up against the wall of the elevator. She gasps but does not fight.

"You should have walked away," I growl.

She giggles, eyelids lowering, chin tipping back. "Why?"

"Because I can't keep it professional. I can't stop."

Kira shifts her hips forward. They brush up against my crotch. There's no way I can stop the natural course of my body any longer. "So don't."

My god, this woman is going to destroy me.

I take her chin in my hand and kiss her harshly. I've wanted this kiss for over a month now. Missed it every moment since I left the cabin. Kira touches my wrist, clinging to me. She wants this just as badly as I do.

"Do you know what you do to me?" I whisper. "Do you have any idea?"

"I do." She guides my hand down toward her crotch. "Do you?"

I don't need to be guided the rest of the way. I hold my breath as my fingers land against her panties. They're damp. I push them aside and dip my fingers between her lips. "Oh my god."

Kira's eyes flutter shut, her mouth parts.

"Dripping."

"Uh-huh."

The elevator stops. I yank my hand away from her and

press it up to my mouth as if I've been thinking. I can smell her on my fingers.

"Follow me."

"Yes, sir."

My body vibrates the entire walk to my office, Kira at my heels. Through the service hall, onto the executive floor, past a few people that don't seem plussed whatsoever that Kira is coming with me into my office, considering she's our top-performing coder.

Thank god.

By the time I shut the door, I'm afraid I might be smashed to smithereens by my own trembling nerves.

However, Kira knows just what to do. She throws herself into my arms, presses her lips to mine, and moans. Moans for all the moments we've had apart. For all the times we've had to pretend there is no history between us. And for the hope of times to come.

And come, and come, and come.

I can't help myself. I want her. So badly. Not just for now. Forever.

Kira jumps up, legs hooking around my hips. I trip back, catching myself on the desk. She laughs into my mouth. "Good catch, Wynters."

"You're crazy," I reply.

"Tell me you don't like it."

I rake my fingers through her hair. "Why the hell would I do that?"

I catch her next laugh in my mouth, spiraling my tongue around hers. *Dear god*, I want her in the deepest parts of my soul.

"Fuck me," she hisses. "Fast."

Don't need to tell me twice. We are under a time crunch. People knew we came in here together, they'll expect her to come out rather quickly, given my usually expedient one-on-ones with my employees.

That's all this is, right? A meeting of two brilliant minds.

A quick one.

I reach under her dress and attempt to yank down her underwear. "Get these off."

Kira drops down and shimmies her panties off while I shrug off my jacket and undo the closure on my pants. She returns to me before I can deal with my underwear. Her fingers dip into the waistband and, with a delicious little smile, she yanks them down and takes my cock in her hand.

My head falls back. "*Fuck.*"

"Shhh. They might hear us."

I purse my lips tightly together. This is going to be difficult. Not impossible, though.

And if it's hard for me to stay quiet, it will be my mission to make sure it's even harder for her. I sit on the lip of my desk and pull her in toward my hips. Kira kneels one leg on the desk beside me and sinks down onto my cock. Her head falls back with a heavy sigh.

I let her lead at first, take it slow, stretch. Though it feels like coming home, it's been long enough that our bodies have forgotten. They need time.

Not too much, though. After all, this is a work quickie.

I pull Kira's other leg to my other hip and grip her ass as I begin thrusting slowly into her. "God, I've missed you."

"Missed you too," she whispers in my ear.

Our hips do the work for a while, breath matching in pace.

If we want this done fast, though, I have to go deeper. With a jolt of adrenaline, I lean forward and grab the arm of one of the chairs facing my desk. "Grab this."

"What?!"

"Do as I say, Kira."

She laughs and follows my instruction, leaning back and grabbing onto the arms of the chairs. "Like this?"

Though she's not naked, her body is still at my disposal like this. The beautiful plane of her curves set out in front of me, draped in clothes I wish I had the time to get her out of. Another time, though. That's a promise.

I grab her hips and push myself all the way inside.

Kira's mouth forms an 'o'.

"Quiet."

"Fuck, that's so deep."

"Good?"

"Yes, keep – keep – *holy shit.*"

I continue like this, pumping my hips into her, enamored by the place where our bodies connect. Her lower lips swallow all of me. So tight and wet. Reminding me she wants this just as bad as I want her. "God, you feel…"

"Faster."

She wants it faster? She'll get it faster, then. I grit my teeth and pump my hips harder, faster. Inside me, a fire is burning, higher and harder with each stroke.

Kira's body bounces. Her head lolls to the side. "Yes, yes, yes…" she whispers tightly. I can tell she's having to hold back.

Drives me even more wild.

"Keep going, keep going, oh god, Orlie, I'm –" Her body jerks and then…

She clenches around me, an orgasm shooting through her body. I'm not long for this world after her, but Kira comes first. I rip her up into my arms, allowing her to bury her mouth in my neck so she can moan. "There you go. Right there," I whisper.

With a few more jolts of my hips, I follow suit, spilling inside her. I grip her hair with my hand, pressing my face into her temple. "*God fucking dammit, Kira...*" One last pulse of my hips, last bit of impotent seed inside.

There's no time for aftercare. But I wish I could hold her in my arms and whisper sweet things to her. Let her know just how much I needed her. How much I appreciate her.

How badly I'll need her again.

Instead, Kira slides off my body and shimmies her panties back on. I wish I could see me drip out of her. Though I know it wouldn't take, I can't deny myself the fantasy.

"How do I look?" she asks.

"Like you just had sex," I reply.

Kira flushes even harder if that were possible given how red-faced she is from what we just did. "Um –"

"Here." I go toward her and adjust the tresses of her hair. When I'm finished, I can't help myself. I lean forward and kiss her forehead. "Perfect."

Kira lets me linger that extra moment, her head tilting to the side in my hand.

I am so tired of denying myself. My whole life I've slaved away to become the CEO of Wynters. And now that it's in my reach, it keeps being jerked away from me, like a horse tempted by a carrot. Why am I so obsessed with a job that will never love me back when I could have a woman who...

Don't jump to conclusions, Orlie. You have no idea how she feels.

"We should do that again," I say. "If you want."

"Oh, I definitely want."

That's relieving.

Kira unwinds from my touch and goes toward the door. "I should get back to work."

I sigh.

"Don't look so disappointed," she grins.

"I'm trying, but..."

"But..."

I give her a once over. Pretty Kira Solace with her secrets behind her eyes. God, I adore her.

"That was nice."

"Really nice."

"Yeah."

She grabs the door handle and gives me one last glance. "I'll see you soon." The door shuts behind her.

I immediately collapse into my office chair and stare out the windows overlooking the Pacific, trying not to be all giggly and foolish. I can't help it, though.

I wasn't the only one who couldn't resist.

Maybe we overthought this whole thing. There's nothing in the employee handbook about workplace relationships, other than they need to be disclosed. I'm not usually the glass-half-full type, but we could be different for each other. I'm not the same as the men she's had before. And I need to trust she's not the same as the women who have hurt me.

This could be something.

In fact, it could be everything.

17

KIRA

"I swear to god, if you ask them to sing me happy birthday, I will flip out," I whisper after the waitress walks away from taking our drink orders.

"They're not going to sing you happy birthday," Dana reassures me.

Harley and Amy exchange devilish grins.

"Then what are they smiling about?" I ask.

"They're just smiling," Gillian says and then thwaps Harley on the arm. "*Right?*"

"Right. I'm just really looking forward to the bottomless mimosas," Harley says.

I'm not convinced. Harley and Amy, the two youngest, have always had a troublemaker aura to them. "I knew I shouldn't have let you convince me to celebrate my birthday."

"Oh, stop that." Dana pats my hand. "Birthdays are important."

"It's not even my real birthday." My birthday was at the end of July. Work has kept me too busy to celebrate. Not to mention, I always try and put it off until my sisters demand

I meet them for brunch so we can all celebrate. Being the middlest child of five girls, my birthday always felt like an afterthought. And that's just fine to me. No need to celebrate getting older in my book. Especially now that I'm twenty-nine. Nearly thirty.

Now, Gillian and Dana are already over thirty and I'd never consider them old or anything like that. But they've got it together.

Me? All I have is my work. And a boss I fucked at work just a couple days ago.

"You'd think we're torturing you, the way you talk about your birthday," Amy scoffs.

"It's my birthday and I'll complain if I want to, thank you very much," I reply.

Saved by the waitress, who returns with all our various drinks. Everyone ordered mimosas except for Dana who is obscenely pregnant and opted instead for fresh squeezed orange juice. "We'll be here a while, so we'll put in our food order later," Gillian says with a smile.

Which then gives way to present time. "I explicitly asked you –"

"Kira! You tell us not to get you anything every year and every year we do, so just live with it and shut up!" Amy snaps and holds out a small box to me.

I take it and begrudgingly thank her. Inside is a gift card to an athletic store.

"You know, since you've started running more, I thought –"

"This is great," I say, forcing a smile. The gift itself is wonderful. But it's the fact the reason I've been running more is because of Orlie. When we were at the cabin, we would run together. And after he left, I kept up the habit. I've gotten pretty good since then. "Thanks so much."

The rest of my sisters give me their presents. Jewelry, books signed by my favorite author, and finally, from Gillian, tickets to a conference for women in STEM I've been coveting.

"It was much better than her original gift idea," Harley says.

Gillian glares. "Harley."

"What was it?" I ask.

My sisters are all quiet.

"Come on," I say and lean back in my seat. "It can't have been 'reducing the table to silence' bad."

"Gillian, since you brought it up, I think you're the one who needs to say it," Harley says.

Dana winces. "Really, guys? Is it necessary to be sassy with each other on Kira's –"

"I had considered getting you a subscription to a match-making service," Gillian finally interjects. "There, are you all happy?"

I usually have nerves of steel when it comes to my sisters calling me out. But that's...a lot.

"It was – I just thought –" Gillian shrugs. "We're all so happy. And we want you to be happy too. And I know being in love isn't everything, but it's..." She practically glows. "It's sort of the best. So, I want that for you."

"Gilly, it's fine, I get what you were going for," I say and then hold up the tickets. "This was great. Thanks."

She smiles gratefully although there's an apology in her eyes, which makes this all that much worse.

"I told her to forget it, because, well –" Amy smiles. "We still haven't heard about what happened at the cabin."

I laugh but it sounds more like a horse's whinny. "Well, what would you like to know?"

"Um..." Amy scans the table. "Hello! Tell us what happened!"

"Nothing. We were cordial."

"Ooooh...cordial," Harley says.

My sisters giggle. I roll my eyes. "Look, you can pry all you want, but I'm afraid you're going to be disappointed."

"You're such a liar," Amy snickers.

"Okay, let's keep things –" Dana tries to temper the mood.

"Am not!"

"Are too!"

"Girls! Seriously!" Dana says firmly. "Please, my nerves are already fried. Can we..."

I grab Dana's hand. "Sorry, Dana."

My older sister smiles and sighs heavily. She's nearing her eighth month of pregnancy and I know it's all starting to become really real for her.

"All I'm trying to say, Kira," Amy begins carefully. "Is that you've had this certain glow about you since you came back from the cabin."

"Yes, well, some R and R will do that," I say with a sip of my mimosa.

"That's not the kind of glow she's talking about," Gillian adds.

I hate to gaslight my sisters by telling them something isn't going on when apparently it's very obvious on my face, but what happened and what's happening between Orlie and me is a secret. One I will take to my grave.

"I know it would be very convenient and romantic, but this is real life. Not a fantasy," I say.

"Awww," Amy groans. "It would have been so cute. If you'd have thawed his grumpy, icy heart."

I resist smiling. I think I might have. He's become Mr.

Congeniality of Wynters Group after making a name for himself as the resident grump. If affection and attraction are the things that transformed him, that does have an awful lot to do with me.

It is romantic when I think about it like that.

"Look, it's Kira's birthday. We're not here to instigate or interrogate. We're just here to enjoy each other's company. Celebrate our sister. Right?" Dana explains.

My sisters all agree and then get to perusing their menus for what they're going to eat.

I already decided what I wanted when I looked at the menu ahead of time. I'm just that type. So, I take my mimosa and scroll through my phone.

When I went to the cabin, I turned off all my notifications so as not to be distracted. So, instead of getting buzzes and beeps, I just get little red icons on the apps letting me know there's something I've missed. Keeps me off my phone, which I'm grateful for.

I scroll through, sipping my mimosa casually. Nothing from Instagram, Facebook...

Huh, that's weird.

There's a notification on my menstrual cycle tracking app. I haven't thought about it in a while. I tap it and immediately feel the blood rush from my face.

Three weeks late?

Holy hell. I'm three weeks late?! Was I really so busy with work and clouded with thoughts of Orlie that I didn't even realize my period was –

I can't be pregnant, though. Orlie had a vasectomy. Right? That's what he said.

Unless he was lying. He just wanted to feel me. Use me.

God, I'm going to be sick.

I might be pregnant.

I remember the mimosa in my hand. *Shit!* I can't keep my hand steady as I place it on the table. It tips over and spills into Dana's place setting.

Dana jerks back. I can't find words to apologize.

"Oh no! The mimosa!" Amy whimpers. "Excuse me, can you get the birthday girl another mimosa?" Amy calls out to our waitress.

She beams. "Birthday?! We didn't know there was a birthday."

I try to get up from the table, but it's too late. A horde of servers encroach around me, our waitress counting them into a rousing version of "Happy Birthday". I can't even hear the singing over the din of my brain.

Late. Pregnant. Mimosa. Vasectomy. Orlie.

This is a nightmare. A happy-birthday-singing-servers-late-period-lying-boss nightmare.

No wonder I hate my birthday.

18

———

ORLIE

A WEEKEND AWAY FROM KIRA HAS BEEN FAR TOO LONG. I've been thinking about her day and night, thinking about what I'm going to say to her when I walk into her office on Monday.

I want to tell her how I feel. What I really want. What I think we could be.

It's not so easy to come up with the words to say, though, especially when I've never been good with words to begin with.

Though I've scripted everything out in my brain, I have enough life experience to know things don't typically go the way you've practiced them in your head. I have to be alright with reality taking over.

So, after my first meeting of the day on Monday morning, I head down to the basement. I need Kira to know as soon as possible.

There's a spring in my step. A smile on my face. And even though my heart beats at a rate I don't think it's ever reached, my nerves are at bay. I'm confident that this is the right thing to do. Kira and I can make it work together. Out in the open with the world looking at us. In fact, there's nothing more that I want than the world to know that the brilliant Kira Solace chose me.

When I get to her office, I take a deep breath and rap on the open door. "Can I come in?"

Kira looks up from her desk. And where I expect to see some amount of excitement in her face, there is only darkness. "I'm busy."

The record in my mind scratches.

Um, what the hell? I can't say I ever expected this. That was my mistake, though. I didn't plan for a worst-case scenario. I'm a cocky son of a bitch, I guess. Don't know how that happened. When it comes to women, I've learned to tamper my expectations. "Um, this is important."

Kira sighs and clicks out of some applications. "What can I help you with, Mr. Wynters?"

"Mr. Wynte –" I nearly fall back on my ass the way it feels to be referred to in such a formal way by Kira, who only a few days ago invited me inside her with the wildest smile on her face. I step into her office. "Are you alright if I close the door?"

"I assume you will regardless of what I say, so..." Kira's eyes fall to a pile of papers on her desk that she begins to sift through.

What the hell is happening?

I shut the door and try to find the next thing to say. "Did I do something wrong?"

"Does this have to do with the important piece of business you needed to share with me?"

"I never said it had to do with business."

Kira's eyes narrow. "In that case, I'll have to ask you to leave."

"I'm not following. What the hell is going on?"

She lowers her gaze. "I can't continue doing *whatever* we're doing. I'm not in the business of entertaining liars."

"Liars? You think I'm a liar? About what?"

"You know exactly what."

I don't. I have no idea.

The walls feel like they're getting closer. I'm getting hot around the collar and not in a good way. "Is this because…" What could this possibly be about? "I apologized for calling you boring. I said that –"

"Oh my god."

"If that's what this is about, then I'll apologize again. I'll apologize a million times if I have to."

She shakes her head. "You don't get it."

"No, I don't. I don't understand how anyone could be with you and think you're boring because I think you're incredible. You're amazing."

Kira gets to her feet and breezes past me toward the door. "Words are nothing without actions, Orlie. And you've already proven exactly who you are with what you've done to me."

I intercept her at the door, pressing myself up against it to keep her from opening it.

"Get out of the way."

"Not until you tell me what's going on."

"*You. Know.*"

There's a fire in her brown eyes that is set on burning me to a char. "I'm sorry. That's all I can say. I'm sorry."

It would be imperceptible to anyone else, but to me, the way her face softens is obvious.

"What can I do to fix this?"

"Nothing."

"Kira…please…"

Her lips tighten. Her brow furrows. "Why did you do this to me?"

I clearly still don't understand how badly I triggered her after the incident in the hot tub. It's impossible for me to understand what deep things I've touched inside her.

Sure, maybe she's being overly sensitive to it. But I can handle that. I want her. I want her to want me. If I hurt her, I'll fix it. No matter how sensitive.

"Kira, let me…" I tuck a strand of hair behind her ear. "I'd never want to hurt you."

Her eyes shut.

"Please." I kiss her softly. Her lips don't give in to me. "Let me take care of you."

Kira stands rock steady. Frozen.

I bring my lips to her neck, a line of kisses to her throat. Her body starts to melt. "I will do anything to fix this. Believe me."

"How?" she whimpers.

I guide her back toward her desk, her hands coming to lay begrudgingly on my shoulders. Not pushing me away. Not asking to let her go.

Give in, I beg through my thoughts. *Give into me.*

"Listen to your body. Listen to what it's telling you." I move my lips down to her chest, sliding my hands up her thighs. "I worship you. I need you."

Kira grips the edge of the desk as I pull her skirt up over her knees. I give her one last look.

"Don't stop," she says, despite a pall of fear on her face.

"I won't," I whisper. I drop to my knees and nuzzle my face up against her underwear, breathing in her scent. Kira cups the back of my head. Welcoming me in. I may not understand, but she hasn't pushed me away yet. I push her underwear to the side and kiss the velvet folds of her center.

Kira jitters. I tighten my hand on her thigh to remind her...

I'm here. I won't run away.

Delicately, I run my tongue along the seam of her center, from the perineum to the slit, back and forth. She tastes immaculate, and the little sounds she's making are music. I press my mouth onto her lower lips and begin to devour her. I will take my time. Don't care if people saw me come in here and are wondering what's taking so long.

I will do everything in my power to let Kira know that I am here. And I am solid. For her.

"Orlie..."

I hum. *Say my name.*

"Can't..."

Oh, but you can. You must.

The tension in Kira's body starts to melt. She curses and lets her legs loop over my shoulders. "Fuck it."

As she loosens up, I can feel the pearl of her clit throbbing more and more. I swirl my tongue around it over and over and hook one finger inside her to tease her from the inside.

"Oh my god. Oh my *god*." Kira's breathing quickens. Her hips start to move into my mouth.

I moan against her.

Her hand braces against my shoulder. "Shit. You're going to make me –"

I moan again with affirmation. *Come for me, baby. Come right here.*

A groan begins at the base of her throat and starts to grow until she puts her fist in her mouth to tame her volume. I wish we were alone, up in that cabin in the mountains, so I can really hear what I'm doing to her.

The orgasm snaps like lightning, hips jerking into my

face, smashing my nose into her pubic bone. I laugh with her eagerness.

But just as quickly as it began, it ends. Kira shoves me away, tearing her legs off my shoulders, and tripping into the corner of her office. "Oh my god, what am I doing?"

I wipe my mouth clean of her and watch in confusion. Her shoulders are shaking. She whimpers.

She's crying.

"Kira, what's wrong? Please. You have to tell me."

"You tricked me. You used my body and tricked me."

A dark feeling creeps into my veins. Now, I'm starting to get angry. I push myself back to my feet. "What the hell are you talking about?"

"You lied. You tricked me so you could –"

"Kira, I don't know what the fuck you're even talking about, and if I don't know, then I can't apologize for –"

Kira turns around, wild anger in her eyes, and seethes through tense lips, "I'm pregnant."

The confusion surges first. This must be some sort of joke. Or a nightmare. Maybe both?

"Um. What?"

"*You told me you had a vasectomy.*"

"I did!"

"How the hell am I supposed to believe that when I'm *pregnant*, Orlie?"

This feels like déjà vu in many ways. I can't go back there. Not to the person I was, the drippy embarrassing excuse for a man.

I won't be fooled again.

"You don't possibly mean to suggest that I lied to you just so I could –"

Kira throws her hands up. "What other explanation could there possibly be?"

I snort with disdainful laughter. "You've got to be kidding, right?"

"No, enlighten me!"

"You –" I struggle to cling to the right train of thought to deliver the news that Kira Solace must already know. "You've been – It's not mine!"

Kira staggers back. "Are you suggesting I –"

"No need to suggest. It's clearly not –" I can still taste her on my lips. It makes me gag. "It's not mine. Can't be."

Her tear-filled eyes break. Guilt, doubtlessly. "How could you even suggest – "

"Come on, Kira. You're a beautiful girl. It doesn't surprise me that…" I shake my head. "I won't be responsible for another man's child."

"Orlie, it's not –"

"I think I'm done with this conversation."

I start to turn out of the room. It's Kira's turn to intercept. She slams her hand against the door, nudging herself in the way. "You don't understand, I didn't with anyone else. I promise. I promise."

"Well, I promise I had a vasectomy. Do you believe me?"

Her eyes tremble in mine.

"One of us is a liar here, Kira. And I know it's not me."

Jaw hanging open, a pathetic gasp comes from her mouth. I'd almost feel bad for her if she wasn't trying to make me responsible for a child she knows isn't mine.

I've been here before. The money and lifestyle look shiny. Security makes people do stupid things. Kira Solace isn't that stupid, though, is she?

Maybe I've misjudged her.

"Please get out of my way, Kira. I have work to do."

Kira slides out of the way of the door, her brown eyes

practically catatonic as she takes in the information her stupid trick hasn't worked.

The second I get my hand on the door handle, I bolt as fast as I can up to the executive floor. I lock myself in my office, have all my meetings canceled for the day, and try to regroup.

All the plans and hopes I had for the future, dashed.

That's what I get for getting ahead of myself. I'm cursed to be constantly betrayed by women and their selfishness.

Work is the only thing that will always be there. That's what my life was always meant to be about.

So be it. Work isn't complicated. Work doesn't make you sleep on the couch at night. Work doesn't make you wonder if it loves you.

Work doesn't fuck other men.

19

———

KIRA

I'm furious Orlie was the one who got to walk away. It should have been me.

How dare he even suggest I slept with someone else? I can't believe he's so committed to his lie he's willing to accuse me of something like that. Sure, it would have been fair for me to sleep around. We were never in any sort of relationship. But clearly, Orlie Wynters doesn't know me at all. That's the last thing I would be capable of. Well, after lying about the paternity of my baby just to get some sort of payout.

I've always been a one-man kind of girl. And when it came to Orlie, I was *this close* to giving myself to him, fully and utterly.

Thank god I didn't. He really showed his true colors.

And they're colors I don't want on my life's rainbow, that's for sure.

I head home without saying anything to anyone. Even Polly is in the dark until I pull into the driveway of my home and send her a text.

Everything's fine. Working from home. Not
well.

And that's not a lie. I'm not well. Emotionally, I'm spent. Physically, well...

Since my mind clocked that I'm pregnant, my body is starting to act like it a little bit. The nausea, the fatigue. It's all setting in slowly but surely. So yeah, I deserve to work from home, especially when I'm pregnant with my tyrant boss's baby.

When I get home, Dad isn't there and now that I'm his only roommate, I'm allowed to go in like a dark storm cloud. Slam the door, scream, let the tears come all at once.

I go to my bedroom and throw myself into the bed, sobbing into the pillow. Haven't done that since my early twenties when my hormones were still raging out of control and men not liking me made me question my entire self-worth.

Joke's on me because apparently, that happens in your late twenties too.

Although these circumstances are definitely dire.

I flip onto my back and look up at the ceiling fan as it whips around so fast you can barely make out the blades.

I'm still just a kid living with my dad.

A twenty-nine-year-old kid. But still.

I can't be having a baby. Not like this. I'm not like my sisters. I'm not strong enough. I've always planned on *planning* this. Having a husband, or at least a partner. Tracking my ovulation, planning it all out to a tee so that we'd be *ready*. No accidents.

I don't want to be like my mom. She wasn't ready. And consequently, she had five children in rapid succession and then gave up. Gave us up. It wasn't something she wanted.

Or if she did, it all came at her too fast. Life has a way of doing that.

I have options. I could have an abortion. Although something about that doesn't feel right. I'm a grown-ass woman. The choice is always mine to make, but it would feel wrong, like looking a gift horse in the mouth when I know this is something I want.

I want to be a mom more than anything. I just wanted to be ready when it happened.

Glancing at my side table, I spy the blur of black and white letters. I pick up the note and read through it once more.

Pregnancy Verification Letter reads in bold black script at the top.

My doctor offered it to me to give to my employer. Signed, dated, and all that. But I wanted it more for myself. I'm only a little over two months. There's no sonogram to be had, no images. This is the only way I've been able to make reality sink in.

I fold up the letter, tear it to pieces, and stick the pieces in the waste basket at my bedside.

I'm not going to think about it for now. I'm not going to do *anything* for now.

I close my eyes and let sleep take me away.

"You have to eat, Kira."

I shake my head.

Dana sighs, the tray of food in her hands cooling off by the second. "Look, I came all the way up here –"

"No one asked you to."

"*Dad* asked me to."

I lift my head from my pillow. "Am I Dad? Does it look like I care?"

Dana doesn't deserve my anger, not really. But no one in this family understands that wanting to be alone involves actually *being* alone.

Dana puts the tray down on my desk and then sits on the edge of the bed. It creaks more under her weight than ever. "It might make you feel better. To eat."

"It won't." Nothing will. In fact, eating might exacerbate things, considering there's been an uptick in nausea the past few hours. Fuck, the morning sickness isn't just in the morning.

Ever so softly, Dana runs her hand back through my hair. Feels nice. "You're angry. I hear that. I don't get it, but —"

"There's nothing to get." I bury my face further into the pillow.

"Okay. I won't try."

I smile. "You'll make a good mom."

Desperately, I'd love for her to say, "You too." But she doesn't know the circumstances I'm in. And I'm not about to tell her when everything is still so fresh. So uncertain.

"Thanks, Kira."

"How's patient zero?" Harley says from the doorway.

"God, you invited her too?" I growl and sit up in bed. I'm greeted by not just Harley, but also Gillian in the doorway. "You've got to be fucking —"

"Dad called us," Gillian says firmly. "You know, we're moms. We know things."

"Can everyone stop pretending like they can help me? I don't need to be mothered. I need to be left alone."

Harley flits in and sits on the other side of me. "Yeesh,

this is bad. There was a time when I was just like you, Kira. Not too long ago."

"Oh god, don't remind me…" Dana says quietly, remembering the time Harley did this exact same thing when she was hiding her pregnancy.

I'm annoyed by the fact I'm not even original. Just another Solace sister not wanting to eat and crying into her pillow because she's hiding her pregnancy.

"So, what's the secret, Kira? Spill it," Harley says. "We'll find out eventually."

"I wouldn't do that unless you want to get punched, Harl," Gillian says.

I glare at Harley. "Listen to your sister, she knows what's good for you."

The corners of Harley's mouth deepen in awkwardness, unsure what to do next.

As if on cue, Amy flies into the doorway. "I heard one of the Solace Sisters needs solidarity, so –"

"No. No fucking way," I say. "Get out! Everyone get out!" I grab a pillow and swing it toward Gillian and Harley, purposefully leaving Dana out of the fray. "Get out, get out, get –"

"Okay, girls, I think she wants us to get out, so –" Dana starts shepherding my fleeing sisters out of the room. "Door closed or –'"

"CLOSED. OBVIOUSLY."

Dana gives me a sheepish smile before shutting the door quietly behind her.

I press the pillow to my face and scream. Why doesn't anyone understand what I need? Why can't anyone fix this?

Joke's on you, Kira. You're the only one who understands what you need. And the only one who can fix this.

But what if none of this can be fixed? What if I'm doomed to be a mess for life?

———

I WAKE UP THE NEXT MORNING TO A QUIET RAPPING AT the door. "Kira, honey...it's Dad."

I lift my head and wipe the crust from my eyes, a combination of sleep and tears that seemed to come on and off all night. "Come in."

Dad pokes his head in. His hair is all bedhead and his eyes are wide. "Hey, sport."

"Since when did you call me sport?" I ask. Poor guy put up with me yesterday being practically mute. He deserves a little smile.

"Since I'm asking you to play ball with me today."

I roll my eyes. Classic Kent Solace dad joke *trap*.

"I have your favorite." He holds up another tray of food. "Maybe this will go over better than..."

We both look at the tray of untouched food on the desk. I'm sure it's all half-hardened glop by now. "I don't know, Daddy. I'm still not hungry."

"It's waffles, though," he says, voice upgliding with desperation. "Here. Breakfast in bed for my little girl."

I force a smile as he sets the tray over my legs. Homemade Belgian waffles in the shape of Mickey Mouse with a whipped cream smile and chocolate chips for eyes. "Man, these do look good." Although the thought of swallowing something makes me scared I might throw up. And then everyone will know.

Harley told me how Dad sniffed out her pregnancy. I refuse to be his next victim.

"I knew you couldn't resist a Mickey waffle." Dad pulls out the chair from my desk and stares at me.

"Um..."

"Eat, eat! Don't mind me."

I don't have the heart to tell him it's impossible not to mind him when he's staring right at me like he might eat me. "Daddy, look –"

"I'm just here. If you want to talk. About anything. About whatever. Seriously. I know I'm your dad, but I'm a girl dad. You know, none of that girl stuff freaks me out."

I grimace. "Please don't call it girl stuff."

"Er. Sorry, just trying to be relatable. Or... You know."

"I'm going to make this easy for you. I'm not talking. I have nothing to say. What's going on with me is for me alone. And I'd appreciate it if you'd keep the girls out of it. And if you'd back off too," I say as kindly as I can.

Dad's whole body shifts, muscles tightening, eyes widening. There was no way for me to say that without totally ripping out his insides. But sadly, it's what had to be done.

"Okay, sport, okay. I gotcha." He waits a second longer as if maybe I'll change my mind.

I don't.

"Welp. You eat. I'll be around if you need anything," he says and pushes himself up from the chair before shuffling out the door. "Anything. Seriously."

I believe every word. I know my dad or sisters would do anything for me.

Right now, though, the best thing they can do for me is pretend like I don't exist.

That's what I'm trying to do, anyway.

20

ORLIE

THE STEAK IS COOKED PERFECTLY, THE POTATOES whipped up like heaven, and the old fashioned I've ordered to drink is the perfect balance of sweet, bitter, and acidic.

But I'm not hungry. My stomach has been eating itself since Kira told me the news yesterday.

Since my world came crashing down around me and any dreams of a future I had were dashed.

You might think I'm being dramatic, but has that ever happened to you? If it hasn't, you don't have room to judge, and if it has, well, I feel your pain.

To make matters worse, of course, I had a dinner planned with my father to go to. And I'm not going to let him know for a second I'm not up for the challenge of being a CEO. I was excited at the prospect of telling him that yes, actually I might not be one of those corporate robots you were scared of me becoming. I might have dreams beyond running the company. Thoughts of Kira Solace might be dancing in my head.

However, I should have known that wouldn't be the case.

"You're not eating," Dad observes.

I look up at my father and give him half a smile.

"Head in the clouds?"

"Is it obvious?"

"Not about work, I hope."

For once, no. "Always work."

Dad sighs. He taps his fork delicately against his plate and then drops it. "Orlie, I owe you an apology."

I raise an eyebrow. "Oh?"

"You know I'm proud of you, right?"

"I can't say I do know that, no."

My dad's gaze falls and he shakes his head. "I think I've done an okay job letting you know how much I love you. But I guess I've never told you that I'm proud of you."

He straightens up, eyes directly on mine. Father and son.

"I'm very proud of you and all you've managed to accomplish at Wynters Group. And how good of a leader I know you're going to be."

My heart leaps into my mouth.

"Just in the past month, you've made so many strides. I was scared to step back because I knew I'd be missed. Not to be arrogant–"

"Wow, Dad, we get it. You're a beloved CEO," I say cheekily.

Dad runs his hand through his long hair. "Look, I knew it would come out wrong, but –"

"I'm teasing, Dad. Everyone loves you."

His shoulders fall. "I'm ready to retire. I really am. And the last thing I want is to step away and leave you with a company that's lost faith in itself."

I nod. "I understand."

"You're still growing up. I know you're not a kid, I

mean, you're in your thirties. But...well, you'll always be my kid, I guess. And I don't want my kid to struggle. So, if I can prevent that –"

"That's life, Dad," I say, a wryness in my chest. "You can't stop me from struggling."

"Yes. I think I'm starting to realize that. Anyway. I'm really proud of the initiative you've taken with your position. Not just with your future projects, but in the way you're starting to recognize the individuals that make up Wynters. They really are everything. They're what make us. Don't forget that."

Despite Kira's indiscretions, I can't forget that. No one deserves to suffer for one woman's mistakes. Besides, I've started to genuinely become fond of many of the people who work for me. I go to watch races with one of the guys in accounting and enjoy chatting with Meghna in HR about her three dachshunds.

Wynters Group really is a family in its own fucked up way.

"So, anyway. That's my story and I'm sticking to it."

"Thanks, Dad."

He cracks his knuckles and then digs into his food again. "Anyway, tell me about what's been going on with your end of things. How's the Leon Prep project?"

Of course, he just had to ask about the Leon Prep project, the one thing I don't want to talk about that's work-related since it has everything to do with Kira.

"Good."

"Just good? You were so excited about it! I mean at that executive meeting, you were talking about how it was going to set a precedent."

"It was. I mean. It is." I sigh. "Listen, can we just not talk about work so I can eat a bit?"

Dad frowns but nods. "Of course, Orlie, of course."

I start to cut a piece of steak.

"Is everything alright with Kira?"

I drop my fork. "What?"

"Jeez, did I strike a nerve?"

"No, I just – why wouldn't things be alright with Kira?"

Dad shrugs. "You just seemed to want to stop talking about the project pretty quickly and I don't want you two butting heads. My son and my favorite employee."

I bite the inside of my cheek. How am I going to navigate this?

"No, she's great." She is. At least when it comes to the project. "You know I try to stay out of her way."

"Good man. You need to trust her. She's brilliant. She's going to knock it out of the park."

"Yes, of course she will." He's so fond of Kira, that I sometimes wonder if he'd rather have her as a child than me.

I can't ruin his image of her, even though I want to so desperately confide in him and ask for his help.

Dad swishes his whisky in his glass and gets a faraway look in his eye. A smile glimpses onto his lips.

"What's that look?" I ask.

"What look?"

"You know, the weird wistful look. Like –" I imitate him.

Dad laughs. "You do me better than I do me."

"I've had a lot of time to watch, that's for sure."

He shakes his head. "Well, don't repeat this, especially not to Kira."

Oh god. What is he about to say?

"She's an exemplary young woman. In all ways. Intelligent, strong-willed, passionate."

"Don't tell me you want me to set you up with her, because that would be –"

"Good heavens, Orlie. I may have a lot of money, but you know I'm not that type of man."

I sigh. "Thank god."

"However, I think you should be."

"Beg your pardon?"

Dad leans forward. "She is the archetype for a perfect daughter-in-law. And –" He sips his whisky. "She'd make a great mother."

I feel like I might be sick. This is much too twisted irony for me to handle. "Okay, you definitely should have kept that to yourself."

"I'm sorry, I warned you."

"In what world would *Kira Solace* be the *archetype* for –"

Dad holds up his hands. "Just something I see in her. That's all. Don't tell me you don't see it. At all."

"If this is your strange way of trying to give me your blessing to *date* Kira –" I say the word "date" as if I wasn't just dreaming of the idea yesterday. Now, it's one of the most abhorrent things that could possibly cross my mind. I know her character now. I can't ruin her in my father's eyes. But goddammit, this is too much.

He shakes his head. "No, it's clear you don't want to. I won't press the matter a second longer."

I drink the rest of my old fashioned in one go and gesture to the server for another. I need to erase the memory of this conversation as fast as possible. My father might be one of the smartest men I know, but he's always thinking with his mushy heart.

I won't make that mistake when I'm CEO.

21

———

KIRA

It takes me a few weeks to feel like I'm not a walking shell of myself, but I make it. Partly due to the fact I'm working from home now almost exclusively. My request was approved without any pushback from HR. I don't doubt Orlie had something to do with it. Why would he want to look into the face of the woman he lied to about a vasectomy and is now gaslighting into believing she's some sort of slut?

The anger has not resolved itself. But I do my best. In fact, I've started seeing Amy's therapist at her behest. "If you're not going to talk to us, you're going to have to talk to someone."

I've done my best to be open with the therapist, but I can't get into the nitty-gritty. All she knows is that I had a relationship with my boss. Any further than that feels like a breach of trust with myself.

Working on multi-million dollar projects in my child-hood bedroom is a conflicting feeling. A grown woman in a bedroom with clouds painted on the walls is almost comical.

However, it's what must be done.

As I sit at my desk going through some coding for the classroom project, my hand drifts to my lower belly. It happens more and more often lately. I can't help it. I'm nearing three months. And things are starting to feel real. From the outside, no one would notice unless they were abundantly familiar with my body. Orlie might be able to notice. If he didn't hate me. But it's my body and I can feel things firming up. A bit of tension in my skin where there wasn't before. And my breasts are starting to round out subtly where there wasn't much to begin with.

Luckily, the morning sickness has been manageable, which means Dad isn't too suspicious. And I've kept the prenatal vitamins in my nightstand, underneath my childhood diaries. No one would think to look even deeper into my mortification to dredge up secrets.

I've decided to keep it, even if it's *not* on my terms.

I just can't deny the yearning inside me for something more than work.

All my sisters have that happiness, a connection outside of themselves that drives them to be the best versions of themselves. To love in a capacity they didn't know existed.

I want that. My heart is practically buzzing to expand.

And after a few weeks of knowing that I have a baby growing inside me, I've already started to become attached.

My baby.

Not Orlie's. Not even a bit.

All mine.

Gillian did it before me on her own. And she was still so young. I'm nearly thirty. I can do this. I have my network, my family. It's not ideal, but it's my life. And I'm ready to accept that.

I trace my hand up and down my tummy to be. We're far off from the quickening. Sometimes, though, I swear I can feel my baby's presence right there in the pit of my stomach. Getting ready to really burst to life.

I push away from my computer and put my other hand on my stomach too. Two hands are better than one.

It should be my hand along with Orlie's.

"You're such a sap, Kira," I mutter to myself.

I should hate him with every fiber of my being. He lied to me. And then didn't even have the balls to go all the way with it. What's the point in lying to a woman about having a vasectomy and getting her pregnant against her will if you're not even going to follow through on the entrapment?

I speak mostly in jest. Mostly.

There are so many layers to this story I can't quite figure out. Why did he do it? What did he get out of it? Is he really just a billionaire who is so used to getting what he wants and just really wanted to be bare inside me?

If that's the case, he's insane.

Still, though. While parts of me despise what he did, parts of me miss him. And hope he'll come back to me.

I've imagined how I wanted that moment to go so many times. Beyond the fake vasectomy, beyond the anger and the tears.

All I wanted was for him to make it all feel better.

I close my eyes. His face is right there, so easy to conjure it hurts.

With my eyes closed it's easier to pretend one of my hands isn't my own.

Orlie's. A thumb ghosting up and down my skin.

Don't daydream. Please don't daydream... the logical part of myself begs.

I can't help it, though.

As much harder as reality will be after, it's already happening.

Orlie kneels down beside me. Looks up at me with his obsidian eyes that have always captivated me. I long for them. Find comfort in them. "How are you feeling?"

"Fine."

"You're sure?"

I just know he'd be so careful with me if he actually believed the baby was his. "You're too worried about me."

"You're carrying my baby. I think I'm appropriately worried about you."

I sigh longingly. *Shit, was that out loud?*

God, how I wish my dream would come true.

Of course, that would mean he'd actually have to love me.

Imaginary Orlie lifts the front of my shirt, pulling it up until it sits right under my tender breasts. He leans forward and kisses my bare skin, nuzzles my not-there-yet belly with his nose. "You're so beautiful."

I run my hand through his thick locks of dark hair.

"Mother of my child." Several kisses to my bare skin. All for us. My baby and me. Then, he lifts his chin and smiles. "I want to take care of you."

Now, the imagination can't make up for a man who is not there entirely. I have to heave myself over to the bed (after checking that my door is locked of course; even in my adulthood, Dad has a habit of walking in unannounced). I dive under the covers and squeeze my eyes shut, sliding my hand into my underwear.

Come back...come back...

My imagined Orlie returns with all the passion and desire he had before I had to interrupt my fantasy. "I don't want to hurt you."

I've googled this. Sex is perfectly natural during pregnancy and, since everything is going to plan, according to my doctor, it would be fine. "You won't."

Orlie kisses my neck as his hands run down my budding curves and then sinks himself into me.

My fingers don't do his cock justice, but it will do for the fantasy of it.

I miss his body on top of mine. Miss the way we fit together perfectly as if we were made for each other. I'd never felt that way with a man before. Like my pleasure was his and vice versa.

Orlie pulls my legs around his waist and continues to caress my body with his hands, one wide palm finally resting over my stomach. "You're mine, Kira."

My body jolts.

Shit, that feels good.

"Everyone will know that you belong to me now."

I move my fingers faster. The orgasm is rushing through me, a torrent of energy, ready to break the dam.

"And I..."

Oh god.

"I belong to you."

The pleasure rips through my center, bursting to life with tickling heat that leaves me gasping. My eyes pop open and...

The fantasy is over.

Orlie was never here. Orlie never wanted to be the father of my child. Orlie is just a liar who thinks I sleep around.

I don't belong to him. And he certainly doesn't belong to me.

My eyes prick with tears. "No, no, no. Stop crying." The crying comes much more often than I'd like.

I want to forget about him completely.

But I can't. Orlie is my boss. And he's indelibly a part of me, his seed planted inside me. Growing.

I feel like I belong to him in the deepest sense. Before the baby, even. It's all I've wanted since the cabin.

And I can't have it.

I close my eyes and tears rush down my cheeks into my ears.

I'm going to be a mom. A single mom to a child who is unwanted by their father.

"But I want you," I whisper. "I want you enough for the both of us."

That much is true.

As if to abuse myself further, I hope it's a boy.

A Wynters boy. Part of the legacy.

Even if Orlie doesn't think the baby inside me is a Wynters at all.

22

ORLIE

"She's running me ragged, man," Hunter says with a heavy sigh.

Axel chuckles. "You're not going to hear me complaining."

I shouldn't have agreed to going out, much less with two members of the Solace family, but when Hunter reached out, I couldn't say no. For one, I want to keep up appearances that nothing is wrong. And for another, well, I thought I might be able to get a little intel.

I'm having doubts. They don't feel legitimate, considering the simplest explanation is usually the right one. And between my vasectomy, a scientific medical procedure, not working, and Kira sleeping around, the latter seems way more plausible.

Still, though. I have to wonder.

"I'm not complaining, I'm just...old." Hunter takes a swig of his beer.

"You're telling me those rickety bones can't handle a younger woman's libido?" Axel asks.

With a grimace, Hutner rolls his eyes. "I was saying 'old' in jest."

I close my eyes. "How would your wives feel if they knew you were talking about this?"

"As if they're not constantly discussing their scheme to become pregnant at the same time!" Axel says. "We're allowed to talk just as much as they are."

I smile to myself. I'm glad to have male friends so open with what's going on. Growing up, everything felt so shallow.

Now, I'm not saying I enjoy hearing about their exploits of trying for children, especially when I'm in my own predicament, but it sets a good precedent, I think.

"I mean, you didn't have to agree to the scheme," I say.

They both smile sheepishly.

"Unless you also enjoy the scheme," I add.

Hunter holds his hands up. "Look, it's a really nice idea that our kids could be growing up at the same time."

"Yeah, it's like built-in best friends."

"Cousins," Hunter adds.

Axel laughs. "I forgot about that. We're related now. Still sinking in."

The way they banter back and forth about the little fantasy of their children growing up together tells me everything I need to know. This is just as much for them as it is for Amy and Gillian.

"And I have to say, I'm eager to do the whole thing, you know?" Axel says. "I missed out on Stella from the beginning. I've got a lot to make up for."

Hunter claps his hand on Axel's back. "You already have."

The younger man shakes his head. "It will never feel like it."

"I never knew trying for a baby was so...complicated," I remark. Not that I've ever tried for one before. Or could try in the future.

Hunter laughs loudly. "Sex right now is like a job. And I'm not saying I don't want it, but when I feel her tap me first thing in the morning, I'm like –"

"Oh, that's the worst. Let me *sleep*."

I laugh. Sounds like they're getting a taste of their own medicine. Of course, from what it sounds like, it will be worth it in the long run, both of them trying for children with the women they love.

I gulp.

"The only respite I really get is when Amy is at Kent's and trying to talk to Kira."

Don't panic. Don't...panic...

"Is she still on her speaking strike?" Axel asks.

Hunter shakes his head. "It's never been a strike, it's just..." He glances at me. "You might know something, Orlie. Right?"

"W-why would I know anything?"

Shrugging, Hunter replies, "She's been working from home. Surely that must have been cleared with HR or something."

Few. "Well, that's confidential, but...our employees are allowed to do what makes them feel most productive. And if that's what Kira feels –"

"Has nothing to do with that, I assure you." Hunter finishes off the last of his beer. "Something is going on. And Kira's not usually so..."

"Complicated?" Axel offers.

"Right! Exactly."

I frown. "How do you mean?"

"Well, look, Kira isn't a big talker, right? But when she

talks, it means something. Because of that, it's usually pretty easy to get a read on her," Hunter says.

Axel picks up quickly. "She keeps things as simple as possible for everyone's sake."

If only they knew... "Come on, Kira must have some skeletons in her closet. Her own secrets."

Axel and Hunter exchange a look before Axel goes on, "I mean, sure. Who doesn't? What I mean is...Kira is the definition of a middle child. She doesn't get in anyone's way and she tries to make things as easy as possible in every direction."

"So, she likes to make things complicated elsewhere, huh?" I lament being the unfortunate recipient of her complicating things.

"I mean, we don't know how she is at work, but I highly doubt it," Hunter says.

I suck my lower lip into my mouth. This isn't going the way I want. I want them to give me as much ammunition as possible to keep believing Kira is a dishonest person who would go as far as to try and make me question my own vasectomy.

"I mean, is that your experience?" Axel asks.

I clam up. It hasn't been. Not in the time I've known her. Not until...I complicated it. Sure, it takes two to tango, but not many people have a boss who crosses a major line.

I made things complicated for her.

"No, it's not," I say softly and then swig my beer.

The rest of my night out with Axel and Hunter, I remain rather quiet as I follow the thread of Kira over and over again.

Something isn't adding up. And I have to do my due diligence.

The second I'm in my car, I call my doctor.

My doctor, Dr. McDib, is an elderly man with a frizzing crow's nest of hair. He's been our family doctor for many years. Whenever you ask him a question, his eyes grow to what seems to be an impossible width before he nods thoughtfully and considers.

He's considering way too long given the question I've just asked.

"Well, Orlando, a vasectomy reversing on its own is extremely unlikely. Under a single percentage point." He twists his lips to the side. "But it's not impossible."

My jaw tightens. "So, you're saying..."

"I'm more keen to believe this young woman is lying, but I'm also a bit cynical," Dr. McDib says and then smiles. "But it's nothing a little testing can't fix."

"Great. Um, great."

Dr. McDib rolls across the room to his computer. I remember the days he was working off a clipboard and taking notes on a sports injury I got in high school soccer. "Now, let me just ask a couple of questions."

My doctor asks all the perfunctory questions, the ones that I always answer in a monotone voice because he's asked them one million times before, but he's doing his job by asking again. "And your urologist is –"

"Doctor Simpson."

"Yes, she's great. Let me see here..." He clicks around. "Her office didn't send over your three-month re-check documentation."

I shake my head. "My what?"

Dr. McDib looks over to me with those scary wide eyes. "Your re-check appointment."

I blink.

"Do you mean to tell me you *didn't* go in for your re-check appointment?"

How many times can this guy say re-check appointment before the term starts losing all meaning?

"Um, no, I don't think I did."

"Ah! Well, that explains it!" Dr. McDib shoots up out of his chair and goes over to a metal tray with various instruments on it. "You didn't do your re-check, which means we have no way of knowing if your vasectomy was actually successful."

"*What?*"

The doctor laughs. "It's just an appointment to see if there's any sperm in your semen still."

"It must have...slipped my mind."

How could I have been so careless?

It's not unusual for me to forgo self-care in the name of my work. Vasectomies are outpatient. I was back to normal in two days. No wonder I forgot about the post-op appointment. I'd all but forgotten about the vasectomy by the time I would have needed to see the doctor again.

But *shit*.

"You're not alone. About fifty percent of men don't go in for their appointments. And usually, they don't have a problem, but *you*, Orlando, are not like most men." He shoves a small capped cup toward me. "In many ways."

I gulp and take the cup. "What's this for?"

"For your semen, of course!"

Doctors are so comfortable throwing around words that make me blush without a second thought. "Um...You want me to..."

"I'll give you some privacy. I'm sure we have some naughty magazines somewhere to –"

"I'll be fine," I say through clenched teeth.

Dr. McDib claps his hands. "Brilliant. When you're done, just open the door."

The doctor flits out of the room, leaving me, the cup, and my flaccid dick. The last thing I want to do is jack off right now.

However, one sad masturbation is between me and the truth.

Let's get on with it, then.

23

——

KIRA

I AGREED TO SUPPORT DANA THROUGH HER LABOR WELL before I found out I was pregnant myself.

Now this feels like some amount of self-flagellation as I watch my sister writhing in pain in the birthing pool.

That's going to be you in about six months, Kira. Better start preparing.

Dana has been in pain for hours and has been pushing for a while now. I'm surprised she's not screaming her head off. But she's so strong. Always has been.

Every time I look to her midwife, she's smiling placidly. Apparently, this is all very normal.

Great.

"I can't do this for much longer," Dana says.

I glance at Amy beside me. The only two Solace sisters to never have been pregnant. We've both been sharing glances of terror the entire time.

"You can," the midwife says. "But you won't have to. I promise."

Drew runs his hands up and down Dana's arms. "You're doing so good."

Dana bends her head back and accepts a tender kiss from Drew. Through every contraction and every push, their connection has remained as strong as ever.

"Alright, Dana. I just need one more big, *big* push and then your baby will be here," the midwife says encouragingly.

Dana nods, her eyes closed tight, head lolled back on Drew's shoulder.

I'd be a fool not to give Drew his due credit. He's been calm, cool, and collected from the jump. Drew has been Dana's champion the whole time. I'm sure Dana wouldn't even notice my sisters and I weren't in the room given how amazing of a support he is.

"You got this, babe. You're so close," he whispers.

Dana readjusts, reaching for something. I hold out my hand and she takes it, squeezing as hard as she can.

"It's happening," she says with a ragged breath.

"Push when you're ready," the midwife replies.

The entire room goes silent except for the grunt behind Dana's lips. I look up at Gillian and Harley who are both sitting at the opposite end of the pool. They are both holding their breath and clutching at each other, eyes swimming with tears as they take in the true miracle of birth. I opted to stay at Dana's side with Amy; I don't need a crash course quite like that.

However, the intensity of Dana's grip gives me an indication of what awaits me in just six months.

Doesn't matter, though. I'll let my sister crush every bone in my hand if it helps her bring her baby into the world. It would be a privilege.

"Good, Dana, good..." the midwife says from her perch at the side of the pool, her hand on the inside of Dana's thigh. "Hold on –"

Suddenly, Dana flies forward with a gasp of relief, reaching into the water.

I peer over her shoulder and marvel as she carefully lifts her newborn into the air. A shocking, brittle cry erupts from its mouth.

And the room alights with smiles, tears, and gasps.

"Oh, my god, I did it," Dana says as she tucks the baby onto her chest.

"You did, baby, you did," Drew says through tears and kisses.

I have a perfect view of the little baby, all scrunched and slick, trying to adjust to the low lighting of the room. The crying ebbs as Dana rocks and coos to them.

I sit back on my heels. It's like the hours of torture didn't just happen. Everyone smiles and embraces. Amy touches my shoulder. I look over at her and see her eyes swimming with tears. I don't doubt she has it in her mind that she's going to be the next one.

But it's me. I'm going to be the next one.

We embrace tightly. "Oh my god, I'm terrified," Amy whispers in my ear.

"Same," I say.

"It's a girl," Dana croaks. "I mean, I think."

We all laugh and, after a check from the midwife, it is indeed a little girl.

"As if we need more girls around here," Harley says, dry-humored as ever, even amidst a slew of happy tears.

Drew embraces Dana and his new baby girl, overwhelmed with emotion.

I can't quiet my jealousy. To see a man so deeply in love with his life...his wife-to-be...his baby...

Reminds me of everything I'm missing out on. All because Orlie Wynters couldn't wrap his dick up.

<hr>

Amelia Young, or Mia as Dana and Drew have already decided to nickname her, has all ten fingers and toes and fits perfectly in her grandfather's arms.

Dad has commandeered the rocking chair in the corner of Dana and Drew's room for the better part of the last hour.

"Amelia is a good name," Dad says.

"My mother's," Drew replies from beside Dana where she rests in their bed. The smile on her face has been uninterrupted since Mia was born.

"An even better name," Dad replies.

Mia starts to gurgle.

"I think she's getting tired of you, Dad," Gillian says. "Give us a turn."

Dad frowns. "Why should I? She's my granddaughter."

"Your *third* granddaughter," Harley laughs. "I mean, seriously guys, don't we have any Y chromosomes to share?"

I have to laugh. Maybe I'll be the one that interrupts the hex of only girls in the Solace family. Only time will tell.

Mia's gurgle turns into a cry. While Dad is usually the baby whisperer, he is unable to settle her down. So he passes her off to Amy. Mia shows no signs of stopping.

"Maybe you should give her to Dana," I say awkwardly.

"No, no. I can do it," Amy says and then hushes the baby once more.

"Here, let me take her. Tana was the same way." Harley intercedes and slips Mia out of Amy's arms. However, she has no luck either.

Dana holds out her arms. "She wants me, I'll take her."

"Let me just try," Gillian says with a smile.

"Dear god, what is this, the motherhood Olympics?" I

say. I can tell Dana is getting irritated. I want to get her baby back in her arms as fast as possible.

Gillian has a little bit better luck, but only for a minute.

"For god's sake!" I march over and take Mia from Gillian. "She wants her mother, obvious —"

I stop. The room is silent. I look down into the bundle in my arms. Mia has completely settled. In fact. She's yawning.

"How did you learn to do that?" Amy asks, a hint of jealousy in her voice.

"I didn't do anything, I just..." I trail off. She's so little. And yet so real. Not mine, but in a way, she's mine. My eyes start to swim with tears. *Don't cry, don't cry, don't cry.*

"She likes you, Kira."

I look at Dana whose stress has completely dissipated now that Mia is quiet in my arms. I try to smile, but all that comes is tears. I scan the faces of my family. All of them on the edge of their seat watching me with this baby. They have no clue what awaits me. What awaits all of us.

I can't keep it to myself anymore. I need them to know.

"I'm..." My breath hiccups. I look back into Mia's wrinkled little face. She pulls her hands up, chubby fingers reaching for what she doesn't even know about yet. "I'm going to have a baby."

No one responds at first.

"What'd she say?" I hear Amy whisper.

"That she's going to have a baby?" Harley says. "Or that she wants to have a baby? I don't –"

"I said, 'I'm going to have a baby'," I say. Louder. Prouder this time. "As in I'm having a baby."

Still, no one seems to understand me. I can't blame them. To break news like this is unusual, especially for me.

I'm the one they can all account for, the one they all understand. I'll always be the same no matter what.

Until now.

"Kira, what are you talking about?" Dad asks, leaning forward.

I look at my father. Daddy. The greatest man I know. The one who has taught me everything I know about love. The one who has given me all the tools to be the best mother I can be. I think. I hope. "I'm pregnant."

"So *that's* why you've been acting weird!" Amy yelps.

"Amy –" Dana scolds her.

Self-consciousness rushes over me. I deliver Mia back into Dana's arms. "Sorry, I didn't mean to steal your spotlight, I –"

Drew and Dana both shake their heads, uttering some form of, "It's okay, you didn't."

I wipe my face clear of the tears. "Yes, that's why I've been acting weird."

"I'm glad I'm not the only one who gets weird when they find out they're pregnant," Harley says.

I laugh. "Yeah, seems to run in the family."

Gillian wraps her arm around me and leads me to the end of the bed. "Okay, wait. Sit down. Tell us everything."

"Do I have to?" I wince.

"You just told us you're pregnant," Amy says. "So yeah, you do."

I sit down carefully. *I can do this.* I train my eyes on my knees and take a deep breath.

I'm not used to the spotlight. In fact, I hate it. Especially now that the spotlight is actually somewhat shocking, maybe even bad in some people's eyes.

"Amy, you were right. At the cabin, Orlie and I...we..."

"I –" Amy's about to exclaim her rightness again, but Dana shushes her.

"Anyway, we weren't careful. Because he told me he had a vasectomy. So, why would we need to be? But either he lied or –" I've looked into the likelihood that his vasectomy didn't actually take. The chances are slim to none. I have to believe in what protects me. I can't be deluded into believing a slim to none chance. "I found out at the beginning of last month. Which is why I got weird. Right around my birthday."

Thankfully, no one in my family interrupts. I can't even look at my dad, though. His face is stoic. Not celebratory. No smile.

I've disappointed him. My heart breaks.

"I'm keeping it. And I know that sounds crazy but –"

"You know we won't think that's crazy," Gillian says with a smile. "I mean, look at who you're talking to."

"But wait, what about Orlie? Does he know?" Amy asks. Of course, she'd have a vested interest. Hunter and Orlie are friends. She's got a little conflict of interest.

I sigh. "I told him, but...he doesn't believe it's his. He's either trying to cover his tracks or –"

"That bastard."

We all look at our dad with wide eyes. He's fuming, hands tightened around the arms of the rocking chair.

"That pathetic –"

"Daddy..." Dana says warningly.

"-- useless –"

Harley touches his shoulder. "Dad, please."

"—sorry excuse for a man." Dad shoots up out of his chair and starts to pace, fuming.

"Please don't be mad," I beg.

Dad lifts his head, the brown eyes he gave me meeting mine. "Mad? I'm furious!"

"It's fine. Really, it's –"

Dad's face grows redder by the moment, ire building in his cheeks. "A man lies to my daughter and then accuses her of lying about having his child? Implying she's sleeping around or – that's inexcusable. It's cowardly – it's –"

Mia howls. Dana and Drew try to calm her as fast as possible.

The fury fades from Dad's face. He looks down with embarrassment, remembering where he is. What day it is. What tender new life has just been welcomed into the world. "Oh, I'm sorry. I'm so sorry."

I get up and go to my dad and wrap him in a hug. He holds me close. As if I'm still a little girl. And I am, at least to him.

"It's okay. I'm okay."

"Kira, it's not okay. No one should treat you like that. Ever. Ever."

"But I'm happy." I might not fully believe it yet, but I'm getting there. Soon. "I'm going to be a mom. Don't you want that for me?"

Dad brushes his fingers through my hair and kisses the crown of my hair. "Of course I do, but – but –"

I can hear it. What he's not saying. It wasn't supposed to be like this. I was supposed to be the one that did it all the right way. Measured and planned without any sort of mistakes or drama. And now here I am, proving some sort of Solace curse to be true.

"God, I hate him," Dad mutters.

I have to laugh. Someone has to hate him for me since I can't bring myself to. "Thank you."

"Of course. I'm your old man."

My sisters crowd me in a big group hug. I hear muttered congratulations, accept gentle kisses and cuddles, and I know they mean every single one.

"If you want me to have Hunter castrate Orlie, just say the word," Amy says, shaking me lovingly.

I cackle. "No need. I'll do that myself once I get the courage."

Harley pats my back. "Good girl."

"Hey, I want to offer congratulations too!"

We all flip around to Dana and Drew. I fly to her side of the bed and rest my head on her shoulder. We both look into the face of her child as she strokes my hair. "It's going to be great, Kiki. Really great."

If my sisters all believe it, I will too.

I'm going to be a mom. And it's going to be great.

24

ORLIE

"...AND AFTER THAT, YOU HAVE YOUR THREE O'CLOCK monthly standup with Wynters Singapore," Quincy rattles off another meeting in a long string of meetings.

The two of us are walking at a steady clip down the hallway of the executive floor. For once in my tenure here, the hall is decorated for the holiday.

Halloween. I've never liked Halloween and I doubt anyone would be shocked to hear that.

There are black and orange garlands lining the walls, carved pumpkins from the pumpkin-carving contest starting to turn sallow, and ghosts pinned to the walls.

I knew I shouldn't have let the event planning committee go overboard. But morale is up. And with today being Halloween, I pray the decorations will be thrown into the garbage promptly Monday morning.

Quincy and I are running late to lunch with a prospective client. Luckily, we already have a black car waiting to take us to the nicest restaurant in the area with a perfect view of the ocean. Fingers crossed the exec is already nursing a strong drink and will let us smooth over this little hiccup.

"Oh, and Trevor wanted me to let you know that you would be, in quote, 'flying solo' today at the Singapore standup," Quincy says as we stop in front of the elevators.

I do a doubletake. "What?"

"He sent me an email last night. At three AM." Quincy furrows his brow. "Is he okay?"

Dad has always gotten his best thinking done in the early morning hours. But that's not the point. "He's not joining me for the meeting?"

Quincy shakes his head and then presses the button for the elevator.

I'm so stunned I didn't even manage to press it. Dad has been easing up his grip the past month and change. But to leave me with Wynters Singapore, arguably the most lucrative of our Wynters Group outposts, is a huge step.

In fact, I'd say it's monumental.

"And don't worry," Quincy says as we step into the elevator. "I've already let them know you're cutting your meeting fifteen minutes short in order to make it up to Silver Lake."

I throw a questioning look at my assistant.

"The Seton Park District Grand Opening Halloween Bash?" Quincy asks, reading directly off his clipboard. "I didn't come up with that, that was the title of the e-vite."

"Shit," I mutter. The Seton Park Grand Opening. Axel invited me over the phone a few weeks ago. I avoided an answer, telling him to send the invitation to my assistant. "You agreed to that?" I ask.

Quincy's eyes widen. "*You* agreed to it."

"I most certainly did not." I haven't seen Kira Solace since I stormed out of her office. A lot has changed since then, namely that I found out my vasectomy did indeed come undone.

Which means it's quite possible – no, *likely* that Kira's baby is mine.

I've known about this for a month. And I'm not sure how to proceed. Clearly, I owe Kira an apology. But every workday that passes, there's still no sign of her. After the way we left things, I can't imagine she'd want to hear from me.

However, that's not the entire reason I'm keeping her at a distance.

I'm scared. I've been here before. And I don't want to get hurt again.

Even if facing it head-on might make everything easier.

In the time I've spiraled out of control, the elevator has reached the first floor, and Quincy has pulled up an email on his phone. "From Axel Hitchins. 'Spoke with Orlie, directed me to you to get my event on the calendar'."

"That asshole," I fume as we march out of the elevator. Axel must have taken my "maybe" and ran with it. Trying to sneak it on my schedule. I'm going to have to give him shit for that the next time I see him. If I ever see him again. Given the way I'm avoiding all of the Solace clan, it's definitely possible I won't see him until the next eternity. "That asshole!"

"Ohhkay, boss, don't worry. We can get you out of it no problem, I'll just send off a quick email."

"Yeah, you do that," I mutter.

I run my hand over my face.

Deep breath. Focus.

I've got a big day ahead of me. Meeting with a new client, helming the standup with Wynters Singapore, and, you know what? Instead of this Halloween Grand Opening whatever the fuck, I'm going to go for a long workout at the gym.

That will get my mind off things.

THE GYM DOES *NOT* GET MY MIND OFF THINGS.

I'm thinking nonstop about Kira. While I'm doing squats, when I'm on the rower when I'm jogging on the treadmill.

I wonder if she's at the bash, dressed in a costume that I'm assuming will hide her budding bump. God, it's been about four months. She's probably showing by now.

Unless...maybe she's not even pregnant anymore. I wouldn't blame her for that. The way I reacted certainly wouldn't instill confidence in someone who has just realized they're pregnant by accident.

That breaks my heart even further.

I could have been a part of things if I hadn't jumped to conclusions about her.

And now...

"Your form is terrible."

I look up from the leg press at my dad. His hair is sweaty, held back in a bright green band.

"What are you doing here?"

"Just finished up hot yoga."

I wince at the thought of my father in his stretch pants. "My form can't be terrible when I'm not even using the machine."

Dad crosses his arms over his chest and he rolls his head to the side. "You've got something on your mind."

"Always."

"And I'm determined to find out what it is. Not letting you get away with that stupid 'work' excuse like usual."

I half-smile. Guess my excuse has always been just that to my dad: an excuse. He's always seen right through me.

"Thanks for letting me take Singapore alone today," I say as I push myself up from the machine.

"I heard it went great," Dad says.

I grab a dry towel from the stack in the corner and start to wipe my arms clean of sweat.

"I wasn't at all surprised."

My heart tightens, warmth blooming through my chest. "Really?"

Dad chuckles at first, but when he realizes how earnestly I asked that, his smile breaks. "Of course, Orlando."

I gulp.

With a step toward me, Dad grabs my arm softly. "Orlie, what's going on? You can tell me."

I take a shaky inhale. My face tightens. I'm trying to hold it all in, just as I've been doing for the past month. And that's evidently way too long at this point. I've never broken. I'm not used to breaking. It's been years...

But now here I am. "I've done something terrible, Dad."

"Whoa, let's not jump to conclusions."

"No, I have. I..." I haven't told anyone about what happened. Not at the cabin. Not in Kira's office.

And it's my dad. He knows how to bring all the emotions out of me.

"Is this about Kira?"

My eyes widen. "How did you..."

"You're my son, Orlie. It's obvious something's been up with you and...well, I just pick up on things."

Turns out I'm not as sneaky as I thought.

"Now." Dad links his arm around my neck. "Spill."

So, I do. We each pop a squat on a bench and lean in close so that no one can overhear me as I tell him...well, everything. Within reason, of course. This is my father after all.

He listens without judgment, a few mm's and ah's here and there, and when we get to the part I've been dreading, about how I implied Kira had been sleeping around on me, Dad throws his hands in front of his face as if witnessing a car crash.

"You didn't."

"I did! Because I had gotten a vasectomy!"

"But it's Kira Solace. She'd *never!* On anyone. And certainly not you."

"How would I know that?"

Dad rolls his eyes. "You wouldn't. Because you're a dope in love and you can't even see your nose for your face." He taps the tip of my nose and I suddenly feel five again.

It's a nice feeling. I'll always be my dad's kid, even when I'm telling him the embarrassing and somewhat unsavory details of my life.

"Okay, so that's why she hasn't been into the office for the past –"

"Don't remind me," I grumble. "But, turns out...my vasectomy didn't take. It's rare, but it happens. So. Yeah. It's mine."

A smile appears on my dad's face and, out of nowhere, he thwacks me on the arm.

"Hey! What was that for?"

"I'm just happy for you."

I rub the spot he hit. It doesn't hurt. I'm just holding onto that supportive touch. It's nice for someone to be happy about this situation when all it has caused in me is dread.

"Don't be happy for me. I fucked everything up."

"No, you didn't. Not yet."

"I don't know, Dad. She hasn't –"

"Stop waiting for her to come to you and you go to her! Are you crazy? Haven't you ever seen a romcom in your life, son?"

I laugh. "Of course I have. *Sleepless in Seattle* every Christmas."

Dad sighs wistfully. That was a mom tradition. It's been a while since we've watched it. Maybe we have to bring that back this year. "Well, if you learned one thing from your mother, it should have been her spirit for life and romance."

"I think you knew Mom way differently than I did," I laugh.

"Well, I have some stories to tell you."

"Please make sure they're stories she'd *want* you to tell me."

Dad waves his hands. "We're getting off topic." He grabs my shoulder and looks at me deep in my eyes. "Go find her. Now."

I FOLLOW MY DAD'S INSTRUCTIONS TO A TEE, FOR better or worse. Most likely worse because I'm halfway to the Seton Playground by the time I realize I didn't even shower before leaving the gym. I'm sticky with sweat and probably smell horrendous.

And this is how I'm expecting to win Kira back? What a fucking joke.

When I get to the lot, my heart falls when I see all the

festivities have wrapped up. Now there are only kids trick or treating with their parents, wearing elaborate Halloween costumes.

The "grand opening" is packed up and done with, leaving only the state-of-the-art play lot and community center in its wake.

You're such an idiot, Orlie. Such a coward.

I flick my mind back to the phone call when Axel invited me. There was something else he said. Something after the playground invite...

"And if you're up for it..." I half remember him saying. "The family is..."

Shit. I was halfway tuned out by then.

But Quincy! Quincy will know.

I'm trying to be less of a tyrant when it comes to running my company. Not calling my employees after hours is definitely a habit I'm trying to instill in myself. However, I know Quincy will pick up. Force of habit. I find his contact on the console of my car and press his name.

He picks up after the first ring. "Well, I haven't gotten a call from you after five in –"

"The invite. Forward me the invite."

"Whoa, whoa, whoa. Slow down. What?"

"For the Playground Halloween Celebration Extrava-whatever! Forward the invitation to my email. I need it."

Quincy is silent for a moment and then says. "Done."

I pull my phone off the passenger seat and open the email.

Yes, there is the fancy e-vite explaining all the logistics of the grand opening. And then there's an addendum at the end, something written by Axel.

Orlie is welcome to join us at Ricks Tavern for a private get-together with my family.

"Ricks Tavern! Yes, this is – oh, Quincy, I could kiss you!"

"Please don't," my assistant says dryly.

I thank him again, hung up the call, and put my car into gear.

I've got to get to Ricks Tavern.

However, as I speed down the residential streets, trying to get to the central Silver Lake corridor, my stomach twists. I don't want to surprise Kira, not when she's with her family. I should let her know.

I should...call her.

I pull the car over briefly and, just like I've done many times since August, I navigate to her contact. I've never pressed called.

This time, though, I do.

25

———

KIRA

YOU'VE GOT TO BE KIDDING ME.

ORLIE HAS CALLED ME THREE TIMES. TWO MONTHS and I haven't heard a thing and now he's called me three times. *In a row.*

I reject each call. I'm busy. Preoccupied, surrounded by family and close friends. Everyone is wearing silly Halloween costumes, including me. I've opted for a classic witch. It allows me to wear a raggedy old dress that hangs in such a way that no one could construe I have a bump even if they tried. However, it's a bit counterintuitive, considering part of the reason this celebration is even happening is because of me.

Everyone here knows I'm pregnant. It's not just the family, but the close friends. The Solace in-crowd, including Lola and Victoria. From there, the connections build in concentric circles to add up to about thirty people in the room.

Gillian practically insisted that this afterparty be turned into a celebration of my pregnancy.

I just don't feel particularly celebratory. I'm going to be

a single mom. Not that's something to be ashamed of, in the grand sense.

I do feel ashamed, though. Cast aside by the person I *know* is the father of the baby, my very own boss who made it seem like maybe there was a future in us...

It's deeply painful.

Still, I'm trying to enjoy these early stages. At least the ones where I'm not aching in some form.

I've made it four months. Past that first trimester. Past the higher chances of loss.

This baby is sticking around for the long haul. My teensy.

That's what I call them. "My teensy". I don't yet know the gender, but what I do know beyond a shadow of a doubt is that my baby is a tiny little thing. Size of a pear.

Although, when I think about it, a pear isn't tiny. You can hold a pear in your hand. A pear doesn't just disappear. See what I did there? Disap-*pear*?

Look, I'm going to have to make up for the lack of dad jokes in my baby's life.

There is the chiming of glass. My dad stands at the front of the room; he decided to partner costume with me and go as a warlock. Although he's shed most of his costume at this point. Getting way too hot in the elastic beard and wool robes. The beard is now around his neck and he's discarded his pointy warlock hat on a table nearby. "I'd like to make a toast," he says, holding up a glass of champagne.

A waiter walks around with glasses of champagne, distributing them quickly. As he plows toward me, I start to feel nervous to reject it.

"We're fine, thanks." Gillian swoops in before the server can meet me, waving him off.

"Thanks," I say.

She wraps her arm around my waist and tucks me into her side. I'm self-conscious she can feel the new thickness of my waist.

"I just want to thank everyone for coming here to celebrate Axel and Gillian's success with the Seton Playground. And an amazing grand opening." Dad smiles. "But the real reason we're all here tonight is to celebrate my daughter Kira."

The room turns toward me. I want to disappear into Gillian's side completely. And she knows it, which is why she squeezes my arm tightly. *You got this,* her support seems to say.

"I've always been proud of Kira's accomplishments. She's bright, witty, and no-nonsense, which in our family is hard to come by."

"Daddy," Amy chides.

I stifle a laugh. Her sass is always funny, but it's even funnier in her little jungle explorer costume. Both she and Hunter look like they're ready to delve into the Amazon rainforest to discover the latest species of spider, The Jessarachnid. I helped Amy sew the eight arms into Jessica's little dress.

"I'm just speaking the truth." Dad looks at me from across the room. "Kira's the last one to leave the nest."

I immediately feel the waterworks pricking at my eyes. It's not hard to get me to cry these days. But when it comes to my dad...well...

My father has been my biggest champion for the past two months. Never pushing me to talk, but always being there when I need him.

I can only imagine how scary it is, me being the last one without a child. Without a man in my life. And now, here I am, crossing that threshold much sooner than any of us anticipated.

Still. He's unflinchingly proud.

"And I'm so excited for the next steps in her life as she becomes a mother."

All the room's eyes are on me. But it might as well just be my dad and me.

"It's going to be amazing," he says with sparkling eyes.

I blink and tears run down my cheeks. Happy tears.

It *is* going to be amazing.

And I'm tired of this shame tainting it.

I touch the top of my bump and slide my hand down, the fabric showing the outline of my stomach if only for a moment.

It's a start. Baby steps. No pun intended.

"So, a toast to Kira and the next great adventure!"

The room holds their glasses aloft. Gillian whispers, "Cheers!" in my ear as they toast.

I laugh, blush. I'm not used to being the center of attention like this. Admittedly, it's nice.

"How's my favorite witch doing?" Gillian asks, pulling me away to a quiet corner.

I giggle. "Good. By the way, what's your costume?"

Gillian looks like her normal self: boho dress, long waving locks. Just topped with a flower crown. "I'm a child of the summer of sixty-nine."

"So, you forgot to come up with a costume and just donned a flower crown and –"

"Hey, hey, hey. Don't be rude. I was preoccupied."

I glance over at Axel and Stella. They've paired up as Holmes and Watson, with Stella pretending to smoke a wooden pipe and Axel wearing a pair of fake glasses and a stethoscope around his neck.

"True. I bet your job was to outsource a lot of that, huh?"

Gillian smiles. "They're cute, right?"

I swallow. *Don't be jealous. Don't be jealous.*

As if reading my mind, Gillian touches my shoulder. "Hey. I've been in your shoes."

"Yeah, but at least not all of your sisters were booed up as the kids say," I say with a snort.

"Sure, I won't claim to know what that feels like, Kira. Not at all. But I was really young and...you have your feet under you. I'm not saying either of us had it easier or better. I just want to let you know I'm here for you when the walls are closing in. Because, trust me, when the baby comes, you'll be feeling the best and worst emotions of your life."

I sigh heavily and touch the top of my stomach again. "I really hope it's more good than bad."

"Oh, it is, it is. It's so..." Gillian looks over at Stella again. The little girl has whipped out a magnifying glass and is peering into baby Mia's face. I'm shocked at how good of a sleeper the one-month-old is. "It's the best. But that doesn't mean it's not hard."

"Did you ever –" I falter. Any time I think about Mom in the presence of my sisters, I feel guilty. Like I'm inviting bad energy into the room. "Worry you'd be bad at it?"

"Of course. It's only natural."

"But like...Mom?" I can't formulate a meaningful question to frame it.

From the look on Gillian's face, though, I can see she gets it. "You're not like Mom, Kira."

"We don't know that for sure."

"*You're not like Mom.* None of us are. Because all of us know what it's like to lose that kind of love. And since we had each other, none of us will ever turn away from it. I promise you that your baby is –" Gillian's lower lip trembles. "So lucky, Kiki."

A couple more tears down my face.

"Please don't question it. You're meant for it. I promise."

I wrap my arms around my sister, catching a whiff of the flowers in her hair. Lots of smells make me nauseous right now, but not this one. It's comforting and safe.

"Also, I want to tell you something," Gillian says.

"Do I smell?" I ask, flinching back. "I swear, I'm sweating like twice as much and I can't seem to –"

Gillian throws her head back in laughter. "No. Not that at all." She takes my hands. "Can't tell anyone."

"Promise, I'd never."

Gillian and I are next to each other in the birth order and because of that, we have a special bond. I've never broken a promise to my older sister in my life.

She takes a deep breath and her smile curls to the side. "I'm pregnant too."

"*No.*"

"Mhm!"

"No!"

"Shhhhh!"

I hug her again, tighter, and find myself hopping with her in a circle as I tearfully exclaim how excited I am that we get to be pregnant at the same time. I thought Amy and her were ridiculous for trying, but now that I'm living it for myself, I couldn't be more excited.

"Oh, Gilly…" I push her hair out of her face, beaming from ear to ear. "I should have known. You're glowing."

My sister beams back at me, but before she can say anything, her eyes dart over my shoulder and her smile fades. "Oh, my god."

"What? What's wrong?" I turn around to look in the

direction her eyes are facing and immediately realize her fears.

Orlie Wynters is standing in the doorway looking like a limp Ken doll in gym shorts. How is it that he can be in rumpled exercise clothes and still look amazing?

Our eyes meet for a brief second. He takes a step forward.

"Excuse me –" Dad barrels past me toward Orlie.

"Oh no," Gillian and I say simultaneously.

Orlie takes a step back. Dad might not be nearly as tall as him, but he's protecting what's his. Orlie should be scared.

"Mr. Solace, I'm sorry for arriving unannounced, I was invited by – "

"I don't care who invited you or when or what. I'll give you the chance to leave only once."

"Please, Mr. Solace, I know there's a lot to explain and I don't have a right to explain it, but –"

"No, I'm afraid –"

I touch my dad on the shoulder. "Dad, it's okay."

He flips around to me with a wild look in his eyes.

"Kira, this is not a good idea, this isn't – it's not right for him to show up unannounced and –"

"He tried to call. He tried to..." I can't believe I'm defending Orlie right now. There's a part of me that's desperate to know what he has to say. "It's okay. I can handle this."

Dad frowns.

"She's got it," Gillian supports with an eager nod. "It's okay."

Another second of hesitation passes before Dad steps aside, shooting a glare at Orlie. "If you do anything to her –"

"I'm not going to –"

"He's not going to –"

Orlie and I both stop short, exchange a look, and then flush.

"Come on, Dad. Let's get you a mini quiche," Gillian says, whisking our begrudging father away.

Leaving Orlie and me alone.

For the first time in months.

"You're a witch."

God fucking dammit.

We meet again for the first time in months and I'm literally wearing a pointy black witch hat. I rip the hat off and toss it to the side. "It's Halloween. What are you? An extra in an eighties exercise video?"

Orlie snorts with laughter. I'm so proud of making him laugh that I nearly forget every wrong he's ever done to me.

Nearly.

"My shorts aren't *that* short."

I shrug. "The amount of thigh showing says otherwise."

Orlie pulls at the hem of his shorts and then clears his throat.

"Um, I'd like to speak with you in private, if that's alright."

"Sure. Let's go onto the patio."

Orlie and I step through a set of glass doors onto the private patio of Ricks tavern. There's a gray stone fountain burbling at the center amongst a jungle of greenery. Orlie and I sit at the edge of it, a good width of space between us.

From the outside, I bet we look like idiots. A witch and an aerobics instructor.

Fucking Halloween.

"So, I owe you an apology."

My eyes widen. That's not what I expected.

Orlie nods slowly as if confirming my silent thoughts.

"I...saw my doctor. And, it's extremely rare, but my vasectomy reversed itself."

I remain silent. *Convenient.*

"I – I – promise you, I did get one. I have documentation." He fumbles his phone out of his pocket (I can't believe shorts that small have a pocket). "I didn't go to my follow-up appointment and I was careless and –"

"Why did you get one in the first place?" I ask, crossing my arms over my chest. I'd wrap them around my stomach, but I don't feel like he deserves to see it. To be reminded. "If you didn't want kids, I'd think you'd be much more careful."

Orlie shakes his head. "It wasn't about that, it was about..."

He lifts his gaze to me.

"I didn't mean to imply you had slept around."

"No, you *did* mean to imply that."

"Okay, I did, but what I mean is –" Orlie runs his hand through his sweaty dark hair. "You are not that person. I know you're not that kind of person. I knew that in my gut, but I was so scared that it was all happening again and..." He trails off with a tense sigh.

Happening again...

"Let me explain." Orlie places his hands on his bare knees, bracing himself. "I don't talk about this a lot because it's – it's hard."

Does Orlie Wynters have more emotions than anger and horniness?

"Years ago now, many years – at least that's how it feels – I was with this woman. Diane. I was young when I met her. That was back when I surfed."

I can't keep from gasping. "You were a surfer?"

Orlie laughs sheepishly. "Yeah. And I had bleached blonde hair."

My jaw drops further.

"Long time ago. Different person."

It's good to know that Orlie hasn't always been this corporate robot. He was a bad boy.

Of course, he was.

"I didn't have direction, just surfing and living off my dad's money. And I met Diane and I was living my life for her. Diane and surfing. That was it."

"Trevor hated that…"

Orlie nods. "Good read. Of course, he did. Despised it. Didn't like her, didn't like the surfing, didn't like the lifestyle that accompanied it. Directionless and lazy. That's how he saw it." He blinks. "In hindsight, it was just a response to my mom dying. We didn't know what to do with each other and – well, anyway –"

Maybe it's budding maternal instincts, but I'd love to reach out and wrap him in a big hug.

After a few more apologies, Kira.

"So, one thing leads to another and I get Diane pregnant." He shrugs. "Like an idiot."

"Oh god."

"Right, you can guess what happened next. My dad flipped out and cut me off and –" Orlie chews on his lower lip for a moment. "I thought we would make it work. Diane, me, a baby. I was happy. I was excited. But…Diane wasn't. Because the second I didn't have access to my dad's checkbook, she totally tuned out."

As my heart breaks for him, questions swirl through my head. Does Orlie have a child no one knows about?

"You know, I loved her. She was my life. And I was there every step of the way to support her as best I could. I was there when she gave birth, I held the baby right after her and…" He looks off, his brow furrowing in pain. "I knew something was off. Looking back. But in that moment I was so happy and –" He clears his throat. A couple of months later I found her in bed with my roommate.

"Orlie...I'm so sorry."

He shakes his head vehemently. Doesn't do well with pity. Who does? '

"I was going to overlook it. I could get past it. We were young. People make mistakes and –" Orlie's jaw tightens. "But then he demanded a paternity test and that little feeling I had in the hospital looking at a baby I thought was mine but wasn't quite sure...well, it made sense then."

I can't help myself from reaching out and grabbing his hand. He might have hurt me, but that doesn't mean I want to see him hurting. Orlie is still buried deep in my heart.

When my skin touches his, Orlie's eyes leap to mine gratefully. I look away. I can't handle that just yet.

"Wasn't mine," he says softly, even though he doesn't have to. It's just the appropriate ending to his tale. "I left Diane, went crawling back to Dad, and..." A half-smile appears on his face. "Became the Orlie you know now."

Oh, it hurts. Right in my heart. The Orlie he became now was born out of a hurt I can't even imagine. Although, I guess the Kira he knows now has been born from the same type of thing. Still, though. He's held onto this hardened exterior for a long time to protect himself.

"That's why it's taken him so long to hand over the company. He doesn't want me to do anything stupid. But then again, he was the one who encouraged me to come here wearing gym clothes and crash your family dinner party so –"

I giggle. Trevor's always been on my side. In more ways than I've ever known.

"And the vasectomy?" I prod delicately.

"Oh! Of course. Yes. I just... The whole Diane thing put me so on edge I didn't look at another woman for two years. Didn't want to get into another situation where I was being taken advantage of for my money. To be trapped into a pregnancy with someone. Mine or not. Then, I realized I had a simple enough way to keep that from happening." He laughs nervously. "Should have gone to the follow-up, though, because now –"

I lower my eyes to the ground. "You think I'm trying to take advantage of you."

Orlie carefully takes my hand in both of his. "*Thought.* It was a defense mechanism. You understand how confusing that must have been for me after believing that –"

"You understand how confusing it was for me that you told me you had a vasectomy and then I got pregnant?!" I interrupt, anger flaring in my veins. "How I believed you *tricked* me? Do you know what that does to a woman?"

He winces. "I think I understand better than you might know. But I could never understand what it's like from your side. And I'm so sorry."

I am quiet.

"I will apologize as many times as you need me to. Because I will never stop being sorry for what I implied or for putting you in a position where you feel like I took advantage of your body. Oh, my god," he turns away, looks like he might be sick. "I can't believe you were made to think I would actually lie to you to –"

"Clearly, it was all just mistakes. We don't have to dwell on it," I say softly.

Orlie swallows thickly. "I wouldn't blame you. For any choices you've made in the meantime. Or any choices you make in the future. Regarding..." He licks his lower lip. "Everything."

"Orlie, I'm..." I take my free hand and run it down the ridge of my stomach, pulling the loose fabric back to confirm what he's been wondering. "I'm keeping it."

Orlie seals his lips together and his eyes tighten at the corners. He nods. I can't tell if it's disappointment or... excitement. "Okay."

Okay? This man hasn't spoken to me in months and just found out I'm keeping his baby and all he has to say is "okay"?

I'm done being nice. He's shared his story, now I get to share mine.

26

———

ORLIE

Kira shifts in her seat next to me. Her distance speaks volumes. I thought sharing would draw her closer to me. And maybe it has, but it's clear that the distance I've chosen the past two months has done a great deal of harm. I should have expected that.

My eyes fall to her hands as they tenderly cradle her tiny bump. I would love to touch it, feel the place where we are growing together.

However, her tender touch is also protective. It's her body after all. I don't have a right to do anything about it.

At this point, I don't even have a right to my very own child. At least not without legal counsel.

Seriously, Orlie? You're already jumping to that conclusion?

It's all I've known for the past decade. All I've been able to do is to stay steady and firm in myself. Be decisive, authoritarian. Brutal.

Not with Kira, though. She doesn't deserve that. No one deserves that. But especially not her.

Mother of my child.

"I wasn't sure at first. If I'd keep it," she says.

"I understand."

"I wanted things the old fashioned way. Which apparently no one in my family can manage. Maybe Amy, but even that situation is –"

She shakes her head slightly.

"I wanted to date someone and have them fall in love with me and be married and have a dog first before a baby and then make it to my mid-thirties before becoming a mother," she explains, head held high. "At the same time, though, it would feel like a slight to the universe to turn my nose up at the thing I want most in the world just because the timing is wrong."

I feel my lips creep up into a smile. That's a beautiful thing, that Kira wants to be a mother beyond a shadow of a doubt. Not everyone in her circumstances would be able to say as much.

"Especially because I don't see someone falling in love with me. Not anymore."

My mind screeches to a halt because she cannot be serious.

"How can you say that?" I've been fighting off loving Kira Solace since I left the cabin.

Kira shrugs. "I'm not sexy."

False.

"I'm boring. A rule follower."

God. Also false.

"I'm too serious. And quiet. And –"

"Don't talk about yourself like that, Kira. You have no idea how people see you."

My mouth dries. I want to tell her how I see her. Magnificent, beautiful, smartest woman I've ever met, full of secrets I want to unlock.

I hold it back. It's not the moment. "None at all."

Kira laughs sadly. "Maybe." Her lips fall. "But I didn't decide this lightly. I'm not someone who invests in the cosmic woo-woo energy of the universe like Gillian or –"

"No, you work with the data and the facts and the codes and –"

"Please don't interrupt me right now," she says.

I wish I could truly swallow my tongue. She's right to call me out. Although I'm sure Kira a few months ago wouldn't have been so confident to do that. She's grown in her own ways too.

And I don't mean that in just the literal sense, although there is that.

"My mother left my family. Completely and utterly. You know this, right?"

I nod although I don't know the whole story. It's just a fact of the Solace family that has somehow circulated within those on the periphery. No one talks about it because why would we? It sounds incredibly painful. An unspoken rule: do not speak about the matriarch of the Solace family unless one of the Solace girls speaks about it first.

Now, here I am. I don't know what to do with my hands.

"Everyone acted surprised, but I don't think any of us actually were. Maybe Dad. But...my sisters and I saw it coming in our own ways. That's what I've come to understand in the past couple of years. And what I noticed was that when Dad wasn't around, she couldn't be bothered to be a mother. Once we weren't little anymore, little in the helpless sense, she felt that we didn't need her as much anymore. Which gave her the space to...break away."

I want to say that I'm sorry for that pain but remember

how Kira demanded I shut up and would rather not deal with being reprimanded again.

"My sisters and I thankfully had each other. Really, we had Dana. And Dana deserves the world for stepping up in the space our mother disappeared from. Over the course of a few years, we'd see her less and less. She always had parties and events, all in the name of public service or –" Kira clears her throat. "It doesn't matter. She didn't want to be our mom anymore. I know that now."

Losing a mother is a terrible thing. I'm familiar with the subject. But my mother didn't choose to leave. A cancer pulled her from me. She held on as long as she could before she had to go. Before I let her go. I firmly believe she held on as tight as she could for as long as I made it known I needed her. At one point, though, I was just making her suffer. It broke my heart, but she needed to rest.

Kira's mother, however, didn't feel the hands of her children holding onto her. She waved them away.

I know what it's like to feel unwanted. Just not by my own mother.

"I've always questioned whether I have some sort of 'nuke it all' button inside of me. That if I became a mother would I feel the same need to destroy everything the way mine did."

I shake my head, still holding back my words.

Let her talk, Orlie.

"But I had Dad and Dana. And I've seen all my sisters become mothers in their own right. Amazing mothers. Loving and hardworking. Willing to give everything to their babies and..." She clutches her stomach and smiles, though tears glimmer in her eyes. "If I'm anything like them, I think I can give this baby a good life."

"I know you can." It just slips out, but I can't help it.

Kira doesn't admonish me. Instead, she looks at me and smiles. "Thank you."

I shift ever so slightly toward her. "You don't...have to do it alone, Kira. I'm – I'm here."

Her smile falls. "Two months, Orlie."

"I know."

"I haven't seen you in two months."

"I know."

"Haven't talked to you in two months."

I sigh. "I know, I'm not –"

"You accused me of trying to entrap you into a pregnancy that wasn't yours. Implied I was a –"

"And I'm so sorry for that, Kira. I'm so deeply sorry. Please forgive me." I won't be able to stand to hear one of those dirty words come out of her mouth. One that would imply she was the type of woman to sleep around, not care about the emotions or the consequences. Which is any woman's right, but...she was coming to me with her whole heart on the line. And I rebuked her.

Whatever ill emotions she might be feeling for me have dissipated. There is a smallness to her expression. I want to capture her in my arms and hold her tight, make her feel safe in her smallness.

"I can't just blindly trust you, Orlie."

"Of course not. I won't ask that of you." I am quiet for a moment. "Can I take your hands?"

Kira shrugs. "Sure."

Again, I get to feel her touch. Warm and electric. I've missed it so much, even in the few minutes her hands have been gone for mine. "I've always thought your hands looked so perfect in mine. Like our palms were made to fit together."

Shit, did I say that out loud?

"That's sweet," Kira says.

I breathe a sigh of relief and draw her hands toward my chest. "I'm willing to work to prove that you can trust me. I understand it won't be easy. I get that it will take time. But I want to be a part of my baby's life."

"We can arrange that," she says. "I'd hate for him or her to grow up without a father. It means a lot that you want to make this work."

"More than that. I..."

Out with it, Orlie. You can't hold it in a second longer.

"I want to be a part of your life. I want to be by your side. And take care of you. And be your first and your last. And love you."

There it is. That 'L' word.

"Because I...I love you, Kira."

Kira's lips part in surprise.

"I've loved you for months now. And I pushed it away because of...all the reasons I could think of. But I can't pretend anymore. Especially now that you're having my baby." I can barely believe those words are coming out of my mouth. "You're having my baby. And I want to give both of you all of my love. Every bit of it."

She tilts her head to the side, considering me with a small smile. I lift her hands to my mouth and kiss them softly, taking it as a good sign that she doesn't draw away.

"Please, I'll do anything," I add.

"If you're willing to go slow with me, then I think I can fall in love with you too."

Her eyes shine like diamonds. That's just how precious she is to me.

"Absolutely. As long as it takes. I want you to be as confident in me as I am in you. Because not a moment goes by that I'm not filled with the love I have for you, Kira. I promise."

"Then make me feel it, Orlie," she whispers.

I lean in, ready to kiss her, but Kira has other plans. She pulls our joined hands away from my face toward her stomach.

My heart beats wildly up until the moment she lays my palms against her belly. The slight roundness of her stomach feels like the whole world in my hands. Because it *is* my world. My baby. And the woman I love.

Kira cups her hands over mine. "The baby is the size of a pear now."

I laugh, but the laugh is split with tears.

"Wow." I trace my thumb back and forth against the swell cloaked in black. I'd love to see it bare, look at the way her stomach is starting to change. But one thing at a time. I can be patient. For Kira, I would wait until the end of time.

"Wow," I repeat.

"Don't cry, Orlie."

There's no helping the tears. I beam, slide my hands up from her belly to her face, putting them on either side of her face. "I want to kiss you."

Kira doesn't answer with words, instead closing the space between us and kissing me.

Warmth blooms across my face, enveloping my whole body in Kira Solace sunshine.

"Thank you," I murmur between kisses. "Thank you for —" I touch her waist. "Everything."

"You're ridiculous, just kiss me."

I can oblige that easily. Our lips slide together, tongues lapping at the familiar places we haven't been able to visit in months. "You'll come back to work in the office, yes?"

"I'll think about it."

"Fine, that's fine," I say with a ragged breath. More kisses. "I'd like you back, though. From a personal standpoint."

"I'd like an office with a window."

"Well, that can be arranged."

Kira grins and kisses me. "Isn't that favoritism?"

"Is it favoritism if everyone already knows who my favorite is?"

With a long sigh, Kira nestles her face into my neck. I cradle her there. Our bodies feel different pressed together. Her small swell will soon change, making this feel even more different. Except I intend to be there every step of the way. Every change will be minute because I won't have missed any of it.

This is my second chance at the life I thought I'd have ten years ago. And I intend not to fuck it up even a little bit.

"You're sweaty," Kira murmurs.

I pull away from her. "Oh god, I'm sorry, do I stink? I came right here and I should have showered, but I couldn't wait another second, and I –"

"No, I like it." She kisses the hinge of my jaw. "Smell so good."

My eyes flutter shut. I hadn't even given way to fantasies about the needs Kira might ask me to fulfill.

One thing at a time, Orlie... I won't pressure her or rush her. But on the off-chance she needs some release, I wouldn't hesitate to step up for the job.

"Besides, I'm the one dressed like a witch."

I hug her tighter, laughing. "The sexiest witch I've ever seen."

"No, I'm not. You're lying."

"Are you kidding? This glorified garbage bag is..." She'll think I'm joking, but all the fabric just triggers the want in me to rip it off of her. "I love it. Feels like this –" I drop my hand to her waist. "Is just for me."

Kira tilts her head back, smiling at me. I've craved this smile for months.

"It *is* just for you."

I kiss her cheek. "For us."

With time.

"Yes. For us."

Long after Kira and I part, my arms echo with the feeling of her. And when I lay down for bed that night, Kira joins me, if only in my imagination.

I will do anything to make sure in the future, however distant, Kira lays down next to me every night. Not just in my imagination.

27

KIRA

"Wow! It's so real!"

I grin as I watch the little girl in the wheelchair reaching out to grab something in the VR classroom system.

"It's like I can touch it!"

Her parents watch on the edge of their seats with smiles on their faces.

"Try moving around. Just use the controller in your hand," I explain.

The little girl presses the joystick in her right hand, her mouth hanging open. Then, she gasps in delight. "It's like I'm really in the classroom!"

Don't cry, don't cry, don't cry.

I rest my hands on top of my belly which is now at a point it's impossible to ignore. Six months pregnant. Only three more to go. My baby is going to be here before I know it and I'm not sure I'm ready.

Behind me is the executive team of Wynters Group. We've invited Lila, the little girl, and her parents, to give a demonstration of the Virtual Classroom my team and I have designed for Leon Prep.

I glance up at the screen which is a live feed of what Lila is seeing. "This is our next step in accessibility. If it can happen in classrooms, it can happen anywhere," I explain.

From the back corner, I see Orlie leaning up against the wall, his arms over his chest. He's smiling curiously at me.

My stomach drops at the sight.

We've been working closely together for the past two months, putting the finishing touches on the Leon Prep project. With my new office on the executive floor, Orlie is able to pop in more frequently and, eventually, became invaluable to the project.

Which meant we were spending long hours together, sometimes into the night.

He didn't like this, given my progressing pregnancy, but I'm not frail. I'm just eating for two and sleeping like a rock.

Besides, I like being around him. Like having him around the baby.

We've kept things innocent. At least innocent for us. We've gone on dates together, stolen kisses. At work, we try to be as good as possible, but sometimes I just need his embrace, his kiss.

We haven't yet consummated our newfound relationship in the bedroom.

However, my body grows more eager for that every day. Pregnancy has made me horny beyond belief. I haven't yet gotten the courage to ask Orlie to help fulfill that need for me. I want to be sure of him. Of us.

And the way he's stepped up, shown me how involved he can be when he doesn't think I've tricked him into fathering a child that isn't his, well...I definitely think I'm almost there.

In fact, after this meeting, we're jetting off to my six-month checkup. Together. This will be the first time he'll be in the room with me. See the baby in action. I don't know who is more excited. Me or him.

Or the baby.

Ever since I woke up this morning, My Teensy has been doing backflips. Just knowing that today is a big day. For lots of reasons.

Sure, there's the demonstration for our executives, which will inform us if Orlie can expand the educational sector of Wynters Group. More importantly for My Teensy, though, this is the day Daddy gets to see them in action.

Daddy. Orlie is going to make a good one. This isn't something I've decided. It's a fact.

He talks about the baby all the time. To me, of course. At work, people don't yet know he's the father of my baby. Except for Trevor, of course, who ecstatically took the two of us to dinner to give us advice. Orlie took notes. Literally! There's a note on his phone for every piece of advice he's gotten from his father or mine. Or my sisters. Or his friends.

Part of loving me is loving my family. And Orlie has stepped up, joined us for family events and meals, taken private conversations with my father which left him completely pale by the time they were over because of how stressed he was.

Dad has told me that Orlie is still earning his trust, but... he's doing a good job so far.

"The more we can focus resources on projects like this, the more accessible we can make them. Not all kids with learning differences have the backing of schools like Leon Prep. I know to many, accessibility has no place in conversations where the bottom line is concerned, but..."

I gesture to Lila who is engaging with her teacher virtually, a big smile on her face.

"I mean, come on. Wynters Group is in no place of depriving all children of the capacity to learn."

Orlie comes up to meet me at the front of the room, a kind smile on his face. "You can join us tomorrow for a full-length presentation on the logistics of funding an education wing. For now, though, I'd like to thank Lila and her parents for coming out here today for the demonstration. Kira and I will be here for further questions as the demo continues."

Orlie and I post up to the side while Lila continues to explore the virtual world of her classroom. As some of the execs come over to us and ask questions, Orlie continuously checks his watch. He's anxious about the appointment. I know because the first text I received from him this morning was, "I'm so nervous," and I know he wasn't talking about the presentation. He goes to presentations every day.

How many times do you get to go to a six-month checkup for your unborn baby?

Potentially only once.

***

ORLIE PACES BACK AND FORTH, ARMS CROSSED OVER HIS chest. His sleeves are rolled up to his elbows because he was getting hot even though the doctor's office is perpetually cold.

"What's taking so long?" he asks.

"Doctors take a long time. You know this," I say with a chuckle.

He huffs and continues pacing.

"Hey, come here," I say, holding out my hand.

Orlie takes it and leans on the edge of the examination table where I'm sitting. I take his hand and put it over the orb of my belly. I can see the relief immediately hit him, shoulders relaxing, jaw unclenching.

"Everything's okay."

"We don't know that."

"Well, has anything bad happened yet? No. So, we have no reason to believe that anything is wrong."

Of course, I'm worried about my baby. Every mother is, especially when they're hidden in the warm confines of your womb and you can't be sure exactly what's going on. However, I have three sisters who have had children to rely on, one of whom is also currently pregnant. They've all been incredibly encouraging, all ready at a moment's notice when I have a question even in the middle of the night about something ridiculous like a sharp pain in my back or my inability to even look at a pickle.

Basically, it's all normal because pregnancy truly is a free-for-all depending on who you are. I've been learning to go with the flow.

Orlie, on the other hand, does not go with the flow. Those surfer days are far behind him. He wants to understand everything as soon as I feel it.

Poor guy. I think he'd be the pregnant one if he could be.

There's a tiny knock on the door and then my doctor waltzes in. "Sorry to keep you waiting! Let's get a look at this baby!" Doctor White says with her beaming smile that lives up to her name.

"Are you Dad?" she asks Orlie.

Orlie pops back up to standing. "Y-yes. Yes, that's me. I'm Dad."

"Aww..." She grins at me. "Nervous, huh?"

"Very," I say.

"Let's quell those nerves, then."

Doctor White goes through the normal questions, checking in with me about how I'm feeling, if anything out of the ordinary is going on. I answer everything and, to no surprise, every symptom or strange fluke is indeed normal.

Orlie breathes an audible sigh of relief.

"Now, you wanted an ultrasound today too, is that right?"

"Yes, Orlie hasn't gotten a chance to see the baby in action yet, so..."

Doctor White smiles. "Oh, this is going to be fun."

I lay back on the examination table, Orlie standing at my side. He watches with intense focus as Doctor White lifts my shirt and squirts the cold gel onto my stomach.

"So, everything's been very, very normal, Dad," Doctor White says, sensing Orlie's tenseness. "Which is the best way it can be. Every time Kira has come in for an appointment, I tell her that this is all picture perfect. So, you have nothing to worry about."

Orlie smiles like a shy boy on a playground. I take his hand and squeeze it. "It'll be great."

Once Doctor White has the machine ready to go, she slides the transducer across my belly, screen only pointed in her direction. She's very good at remaining stoic on the off chance she has to deal with something hard to see. But I'm not worried.

Orlie, on the other hand, isn't very patient. "Is everything okay?"

"Takes a minute. Even bigger babies can be shy," Doctor White says.

"Takes after me, I guess," I say, rubbing my thumb into the back of Orlie's hand.

"Here we go." Doctor White turns the screen toward us.

On the screen is a three-dimensional image of our baby

cast in amber with highlights and shadows dappling their little face. Nose, lips, eyes…It's all there. Looks like a real baby.

"That's…" Orlie's face goes slack. "Seriously, that's our –"

I nod, grinning.

"It looks like a real baby."

"It *is* a real baby," I reply.

"I know, but I mean…" He trails off as he watches the ultrasound. Baby moves one of their hands up toward their face. Orlie's face scrunches together. "Oh, my gosh, it's amazing."

I kiss his hand and beam up at him. Yes, the baby is beautiful and amazing. But Orlie's adoration is something special. It's the thing that's been drawing me closer to him for the past two months. Making it hard to stay away even though there's a logic center in my brain saying, "Don't move too fast, he might hurt you again."

I know this has much less to do with logic and more to do with trying to keep myself from getting hurt.

"You want to know the gender?" Doctor White asks.

I bite my lower lip.

"It's your call, Kira," Orlie says, although his eyes dart away from mine.

"You want to know, don't you?"

He hesitates. "It's up to –"

"Orlie…it's just as much your baby as it is mine. Do you want to know what we're having?"

He looks at the doctor nervously. "Yes, please."

"So polite. Alright. Give me a second to get a better angle."

I'd refused to learn the gender at my five-month appointment. I'm assuming I'm having a girl and that will be that. After all, look at the make-up of my family. Also, though, it didn't feel right to make the decision without Orlie.

I meant when I said the baby is as much his as mine. It's not only the truth, but it's the way my heart has grown to feel.

I was ready to do this all on my own. Yet, he's made it clear I don't have to.

And now that he's here with me, I don't want to do it alone. I want him here every step of the way.

"You're having a boy."

I nearly leap off the table in shock. "What?!"

Orlie laughs.

"Are you sure?"

"Do you want me to show you?" Doctor White says. "Because there's a way I can show you just how sure I am."

I can barely believe it. "All my sisters have girls."

"Well, it was time for someone to break the mold, huh?" Orlie says.

I look up at him. "Are you happy?"

"Of course, Kira. No matter what, I would have been happy. But I know you'll make a perfect boy mom," he says, stroking my cheek.

I flush.

Will I? I'm so familiar with how girls work. And I'm not even in a full-fledged "I love you" relationship with my baby's – my son's father. Do I know a pin about how to take care of a boy?

"Baby looks great. Everything is within percentile to continue growing right on track." Doctor White tilts her head to the side. "Let's check back in at your next appointment to see if he's working his way head down. Right now he's presenting breech. But there's plenty of time to get into position for birth."

I wince at even the mention. There is, of course, the fear of the massive amounts of work and pain that will go into getting my baby earthside. However, more than that, I don't want to rush through these last three months. I want to savor them. My little baby boy nestled inside me perfectly cared for and nurtured.

Orlie and I have three months to get our acts together before we have a party of three. I want to make sure we're completely ready for our little one to be welcomed into a home of trust and love.

I'm almost there with him. I can feel it.

Now, I just need to decide to take the leap into loving Orlie.

ON TOP OF EVERYTHING, ORLIE DOES HIS BEST TO MAKE me feel cared for. After the appointment, he takes me back to his beautiful home in Santa Monica and orders me all the Chinese food I could possibly want.

I sit like a queen on a throne in a comfy chair looking out the floor-to-ceiling windows at the ocean as the sun sets. It might be Winter, but we still have beautiful sunsets in LA.

With a carton of lo mein perched on my belly, I eat while Orlie kneels at my feet and massages them with the mastery of a reflexologist.

"Mmm..." I moan.

"Did I hit the spot?" he asks with a smile.

"I don't know if it was the foot massage or the lo mein, but whatever it is..." I lean my head back and sigh.

Orlie's hands slide up from the soles of my feet to my calves. He caresses them. "This alright?"

"Yes. Feels amazing."

He chuckles. "Good."

I watch him as he works with precision and intensity.

"You're too good to me."

"You're joking, right?" Orlie shakes his head. "You're carrying my baby. I could never do anything for you to match that."

"Well, it was an accident, so don't give me too much credit."

Orlie doesn't reply, continuing the work on my calves. Then my ankles. His fingers work in easy circles.

"Mm. That's nice."

He doesn't say anything for a while and we descend into a silence. Not quite comfortable. Not yet. There's still so much tension, so much unsaid. Silences are still filled with potential.

"Thank you," he says in a quiet, low voice.

I consider him for a moment. "For what?"

"For including me today," he says as he gets another squirt of body lotion to continue massaging my feet.

"Of course. Thank you for coming."

My body feels hot all of a sudden.

Orlie lifts his eyes. His arm muscles bulge as he works on my feet. "I never thought I'd have this."

I frown.

"I thought I had a vasectomy and that was it." He inhales. Shaky. "I didn't picture ever having a child after everything that happened.... Because it broke me, Kira. To think I had this little part of me in the world and then to have it taken all away like that."

I put my lo mein to the side and lean my head in my hand. "Of course. I can only imagine."

"'So, whatever happens here with us, it's..." Orlie swallows. "It's everything to me. Our baby. Our *son* –" He cuts himself off with a tear-filled laugh.

As best I can, given my very protruding bump, I lean forward and wrap Orlie in my arms.

"Please don't take it away from me," he brokenly whispers.

"What makes you think I'm going to do that?" I ask.

Orlie hangs onto me desperately. "I don't know, I just can't lose you. Either of you. You don't have to give me anything else. Don't have to be with me, don't have to love me, just –"

"But I do," I say, cutting him off.

Orlie stops and pulls back. "What did you say?"

I've been working toward this. Orlie is not hard to love. But I feel like *I'm* hard to love. I can barely believe he has thrown himself into me with the passion and ardor of all the stars in the universe, even when I never offered him love in return.

If a man wants to, he will. And Orlie has made that quite clear.

But for me? Mousey Kira Solace? The quiet one with the glasses?

Apparently, I'm worth it. And it's time I finally believe that.

"I love you, Orlie," I say and then touch his chin with my thumb. "*Orlando*."

A lopsided smile creeps over his face. "Seriously?"

I nod. "I want...I want to be with you. I want to make a family with you. A real one." I brush my lips along his cheekbone. "I'm ready."

"Gosh, I want to just grab you and kiss you, but my hands have been all over your feet and there is just something about feet that ruins the romance and –" Orlie rambles.

"Go wash your hands and then come back and kiss me," I say with a laugh.

Orlie rushes across the sprawling living area to the open-concept kitchen, all black and stainless steel. I push myself up to standing and meet him halfway as he rushes back to me, swooping me up in his arms and kissing me with his whole self.

Our son flips inside me. He knows just how important this moment is and I'm so glad we can share it with him.

One of Orlie's hands drifts to my belly. He spreads his wide palm against it as his lips curl into a smile against mine. "God, I love you," he whispers. "I love you, I love you, I love you…"

He kisses every inch of my face with care, a topographer sketching out a map. Like he must know every inch, texture, crevice, all of it, so that he'll never forget.

I find my lips on his again, a deep kiss, tongue delving into his mouth. We have kept things rather tame as we navigate our new relationship as future co-parents, potential lovers. Now, though, my tingling nerves need to be satisfied. I want Orlie's hands all over my body. Want him to see me in a way he hasn't in many months.

"Please, I want you," I say into his mouth. "Take me to your bed. Please."

Orlie's too stunned to take the lead, so I grab his hand and pull him up the floating stairs to the master bedroom. Never been in it, except for the one time Orlie gave me a tour a month and change ago and we both nervously laughed about it, before pretending it had never happened.

"I don't want to hurt you."

I resist bringing up his time with Diane. Surely he must have pleasured her while she was pregnant. Or maybe he's blocked all that out of his memory. I can't blame him for that.

"You won't. I need this." I untuck his shirt and begin undoing all the buttons.

As I do so, Orlie's dark eyes fix on mine; he drives me toward the edge of the bed and, just as my legs hit the end of the mattress, his shirt is unbuttoned, exposing his broad, toned chest.

Delicious.

I slide my hands across his pecs. "I've missed this."

He grins and then goes to push my shirt up, pausing before touching me. "May I?"

I smile. So careful with me. Too afraid to mess this up. I pull up the front of my shirt, exposing my bare belly to him. Orlie's fingers tentatively stroke the skin. He hasn't been allowed to touch me like this. Not yet. And, consequently, he looks at me for permission.

I give him a small nod. As his hand settles on my bare belly, our son jabs his way toward Orlie's palm.

"Hey, little guy," he says. "Join the party."

I brush my hand through Orlie's hair as he leans down to kiss the bare skin.

"Oh god," he mutters. "This is...this is the best."

A flutter of kisses across my abdomen leads me down to the bed. I lay back as Orlie languishes his mouth across my stomach. Meanwhile, his hands start to pull on the waistband of my pants, leaving me bare and naked to the air. My hips buck. It's been so long. And I'm aching for release.

"You smell amazing," he whispers, looking down at me.

"Get inside me," I say. "Now."

Orlie's eyes go wide. Darker than dark. Nearly black. He steps out of his own pants, revealing his hardness in his briefs.

"God, I've missed you," I say.

"Yeah, we get it, you love me for my dick." He takes his briefs off, exposing his erect cock.

I sigh blissfully and slip my legs around his hips pulling him toward me. "No, I love you for all of you, Orlie. Every bit of you."

He sinks inside me a moment later.

"But your dick is certainly a plus." I choke out the words and then moan, stretching around him.

Dear fucking god it's been too long.

Orlie stands at the end of the bed and begins to thrust in and out of me, slow and steady. "This alright?"

"I'm not made of porcelain, Orlie," I say.

Sure, I have several more inches around my waist. But I'm not that different. I still have needs. I pull his hips as close to me as they'll go and groan.

Orlie shudders, grabbing my hips tightly. "Oh, my god."

"Go, go, go, please," I hiss. "I'm so – I need –"

"You'll get what you need. Always, Kira. Always."

Orlie makes good on this promise immediately. He creates a steady rhythm in and out of me, rubbing against the most sensitive point inside me. "God, you're so fucking beautiful..." He reaches down and slides his hand across my belly.

That sends sparks of arousal through me in a way I've never felt. "Keep touching me there."

"No problem."

One hand on my thigh, one hand on my swell, Orlie continues fucking me, harder and harder, until he can't seem to hold onto steadiness anymore.

Our conjoining is erratic, shaking, needy. It's been so long. But our bodies remember.

And after a short, frantic fight for our lives, we come simultaneously, hard and pulsating. Moans and groans intertwine, shaking the world around us.

Afterward, Orlie curls up beside me, slides his hand over my belly. "You're alright? Both of you?"

I cup his hand over my belly. "Yes. Better than alright," I say and kiss him. "Because I love you."

"Say it again."

"I love you."

Orlie's eyes roll back in bliss before he presses his face into my neck. "I love you. I've loved you."

I smile. Because I've loved him too. For a while. He was just brave enough to say it first.

Now, here we are. And I'm never going to hold back from an "I love you" ever again.

28

ORLIE

TWO MONTHS LATER...

"We'd like to invite the happy couple onto the dance floor for their first dance."

Dana and Drew float up to the dance floor and begin to sway together as the band starts to play a lilting Beatles song.

I reach my arm around Kira in her chair beside me and gently massage her shoulder. She smiles at me, the apples of her cheeks blushing. "How are you feeling?" I ask softly.

"Pregnant," she says, glancing down at the swell of her belly.

"Fair," I say and then rest my other hand on the top of her eight-month belly. Every time I think it's impossible she could get bigger, she does. Still three weeks to go until she's reached the forty-week mark.

"Well, you are the most beautiful woman in the room, if that helps anything."

Kira beams and rests her head on my shoulder. It's not even a lie. When she was standing up at the altar with all her sisters, she was clearly the most radiant in every way.

Her teal dress hugs all her curves perfectly, her belly being my favorite, of course. And, she didn't even have to step out to pee, which was her biggest fear.

We watch as her eldest sister and new husband share their first dance as a married couple. "What would our song be?" Kira asks.

My heart turns into a fist. We've been in an official relationship for two months. Marriage right now seems rash.

"Don't freak out, I'm just asking," Kira says dryly, reading my mind.

I try to laugh. I've tried to avoid ever imagining getting married to anyone after Diane. But in all honesty, I could picture this with Kira.

Just not too fast. Let's get a baby into the world first and then we can talk. "I don't know, maybe something to do with hating each other's guts."

Kira scoffs and smacks my chest with the back of her hand. "You're so mean. You want our son to know you hated me?"

"Let's be clear, I *never* hated you. Never, ever, ever."

"Good," she says, snuggling into my chest.

I kiss the side of her head and then smile over at her father who is across the table from me, holding baby Mia who is spitty gurgling. She's gotten so big so quickly. I have that in store for me sooner than later. Although, I'm not trying to rush anything.

Kent gives me a nod and a soft smile. I've done everything I can to get in his good graces the past couple of months and I feel like I'm close to being accepted into his fold. I'm sure a proposal would really solidify that.

The music changes a moment later to another ballad and the band leader announces, "Dana and Drew would like to invite their family members to join them on the dance floor."

Our entire banquet-length table stands, including the kids.

I help Kira up out of her seat. I've gotten better at not treating her with kid gloves, but she is at the point where getting up is becoming more of a hassle. On top of this, there was no way I was letting her wear high heels to this, not that she particularly wanted to, given how swollen her feet have gotten. So, she is quite dainty compared to me. Save her growing belly.

Hand in hand, we sweep onto the dance floor. I pull her as close as I can and we begin our dance.

"Ah, I'm getting déjà vu," I say.

"Can you believe that was less than a year ago?"

I scoff. "No, I can't. That's...crazy."

"Things change when you least expect them to, I guess," Kira says with a soft smile.

"Yeah, I'm the CEO of a company now," I say.

She pouts. "Not what I meant."

I laugh. "Oh, did you mean – did you mean the –" I point to her belly.

"You're so rude."

"Hey, hey, hey. I'm teasing you," I say, then lean in, giving her a kiss on her jaw. "You know I am. You're the best thing that ever happened to me. Have I told you that recently?"

Just this morning, I know I did.

Kira smiles. "Not recently enough."

"Ah, well, I'm so sorry. I'll make sure to say it every hour on the hour."

"That will do, I think."

At Hunter and Amy's wedding, this dance was intense.

Something was budding between us. Now, something has quite obviously grown. Not just our baby, but our love.

This dance is intimate. Not just sensual. But a prelude of much more closeness to come.

We fall into a steady rhythm. Back and forth, back and forth. Hypnotic. Feels like living in a dream. The love of my life, our baby, and –

"Oh god," Kira mutters.

"Wha –" Before I can see what's up, I slip on the floor, narrowly steadying myself from falling flat on my face. "Jesus Christ, what was –"

Kira splits away from me and pulls her skirt up revealing a puddle on the ground. "Oh no."

"Hey, it's okay," I say.

Did she pee herself? I mean, the baby's feet have been pressing on her bladder for a week now, so it's understandable. "Let's get you to a bathroom and –"

She shakes her head, blood draining from her face. "I didn't pee, Orlie. That wasn't..."

As she trails off, I catch up. I shake my head. "No. Are you sure?"

"I swear, I didn't –"

"You think your water broke?" I say in a tense whisper.

Kira's breathing starts coming faster and faster.

"You haven't – you haven't felt anything, right?" I ask.

She shakes her head, eyes welling with tears. "Nothing, not even Braxton Hicks or –" Kira slides her hand under her belly. "It's too soon. He still has three weeks."

I have to be strong for her. I can't let her know I'm terrified.

"Orlie, he's not in the right position. He's breech, he hasn't shifted yet," she says, lower lip warbling.

I wrap my arm around her. "It's going to be okay. I promise. We have to go, alright?"

Harley hurries over. "Is everything okay?"

"My water –" Kira tries to explain, but her breathing can't steady.

I rub her back. "Breathe. You have to breathe, honey."

"Oh, shit," Harley says, pressing her hands over her mouth. "Okay, this is okay." She takes her sister's hand. "Orlie will take you to the hospital and –"

"Yeah, I will," I say although I'm starting to shake. I don't know how I'll drive when I'm shaking like this.

Harley touches my back. "I'll clean this up and keep everyone calm. You go, okay?"

"Thank you, thank you," I mutter and lead Kira off the dance floor.

As we wade through the crowd, Kira starts mumbling to herself, "This isn't possible, I haven't had one contraction, I haven't –"

"Hey, what's going on?" My dad appears suddenly at my side.

I don't stop walking. "Kira's water broke."

"Oh! Oh no. Alright –"

"Don't say 'oh no'," Kira whimpers. "Oh, my god, please don't say –"

Dad swings around to grab her other arm. "It's alright. I meant 'oh no' like 'oh no, what timing' not –" He looks at me with nervous eyes.

Before I can respond, Kira gasps and clutches her belly.

"Contraction?" I ask.

She nods, squinting her eyes closed. "It's intense," she says through grit teeth.

"This is happening too fast," Dad murmurs to me. "We have to get her to the hospital."

Stay strong, don't crack, stay strong, don't break. "Will you drive us? I don't think I can – I'm too –"

There is no hesitation. My father holds out his hand. "Give me your keys. Let's go have a baby."

29
——

KIRA

I blink my eyes open. My mouth is dry. I try to create some saliva by smacking my lips.

Everything below my waist aches. Distantly.

Mm. What happened?

My baby. Oh god, my baby.

I reach down to my stomach, but it's like moving through molasses. When I finally make it, I squish a part of my stomach and...

No, something is wrong. This is wrong. It's too soft. And it hurts.

Where is he?

The last thing I remember was making it into a hospital bed, contractions piling up on each other, reaching for Orlie, hearing doctors squabbling with concern that there was too much blood, and then a nurse with kind eyes leaning over me to explain something.

I try to breathe deeply. It's hard with the pain in my core. But eventually, as my eyes slide across the ceiling, my neck starts unlocking too.

I look to one side. It's blurry but I can make out the

rough images. Just a hospital. Equipment. An IV. I can now feel it in my arm, that tiny needle and tape on my skin. Then, I look the other way.

All the fears abate when I see Orlie sitting in a big leather chair, a tiny bundle on his chest. I try to open my mouth to call out his name, but my mouth is still too dry to be able to form words.

Patience, Kira.

Orlie looks exhausted. His hair is sticking out in all directions. God, what time is it? How long have I been out?

His dress shirt is unbuttoned halfway, and our little one is skin-to-skin with him. I try to smile. The corners of my mouth hurt. Dry.

Orlie pats the backside of our baby, trying to look into his little face.

I want to see him. I want a good look at him.

I feel so empty without him.

"Orlie."

Orlie's eyes shoot to me. "Oh, my god," he says. "Oh my –"

"My glasses, can you –"

He fumbles to get my glasses on my face with one hand.

"Is he okay?" I don't know what happened and I don't care. I need my baby.

"He's perfect. He's..." Orlie leans over to the side of the bed and cradles the baby in his arms so I can see him.

Scrunched little red face, lips slick with saliva, puffy cheeks. Perfect.

"Ten fingers, ten toes. And he's huge. Seven pounds, two ounces."

I breathe a sigh of relief. "Can I –"

"Here..." Orlie places our son in my arms gently,

helping me position my arms and support his head as my strength comes back. "Owen, this is Mommy."

My heart sings.

Mommy. Holding her little Owen.

Owen babbles for a moment before settling into the strange bed of my chest. "Oh, it's okay, it's me, baby, it's…"

I can't believe it. I'm a mother. "How long was I…"

"We got here at around eleven and…" Orlie glances at his watch. "Nearly nine now."

"Oh, Owen, honey, I'm sorry it took me so long," I say with a smile, a couple of tears running down my cheeks. "I'm here now. I'm right here."

Orlie touches my leg and rubs it. "You had to have an emergency c-section. And there were some complications. He was breech and you started bleeding and…" He clears his throat. "Your placenta ruptured. It was so scary, Kira."

"I'm sorry."

"No, don't apologize. How could you apologize for –" Orlie half laughs. "I just thought I might lose you. I thought I'd have to do it by myself." He lowers his head and shakes it.

I tighten my arms around Owen. "But you don't. I'm right here."

Orlie looks back at me. He smiles. "You two look perfect together."

"Do we? I feel like I have some catching up to do," I say, rocking my little one.

"You'll be caught up in no time." Orlie pushes some hair out of my face and cups my cheek.

I trace the line of Owen's nose and then the space under his eyes. "Wow. He's amazing."

"Amazing. Looks just like you."

I snort. "You can't see that yet."

"Maybe I'm trying to put that out in the universe so he takes after you more than me."

"You're an idiot. Now kiss me."

Orlie laughs and then kisses me delicately. He doesn't pull away, lingering there. Lips near my own. "I want to marry you."

My insides twist. "Are you on drugs right now or am I?"

"No, I know we talked about waiting. But…" He clears his throat. "When I thought about living life without you. Taking care of our son without you. Having to remember you as the woman I loved. But not my wife…it killed me. Upon already killing me." Orlie slides his hand over mine so together, we both are holding our boy, together. "I'm not going to rush you. I know there's a lot of things to take care of before that."

We both laugh, glancing at Owen. He blinks up at us.

"But my intention is to one day be your husband. If you'll have me."

I intertwine my fingers with his. "Of course. Us against the world."

"The three of us."

We kiss once more. Our son squalls. "Oh, sorry, little one," I say and kiss his forehead. "You need attention, huh? Well, mommy and daddy have it."

Orlie nuzzles my cheek. "Owen's mom and dad. I like the sound of that."

As soon as the doctor clears me to have visitors, the Solace and Friends parade begins. Our fathers first. Dad supports Trevor through the first grandchild feels.

"I told myself I wouldn't cry," Trevor says, though the tears are already shining.

Dad shakes his head. "You cry your eyes out, Trevor. That's the way it's supposed to be.

They both remark how he looks like me, to which Orlie waggles his eyebrows in an "I was right" way. I roll my eyes.

Gillian arrives next. At five months with her second, she's grown immensely. Axel and Stella follow.

"Oh, let me see, let me see –" Gillian peers into my arms. Immediately, she's choked up. "Kira, he looks –"

"Don't you dare say, 'Just like you'," I interrupt.

Gillian's eyebrows jump and she looks down at Stella who shrugs. "Okay, I won't."

Orlie laughs.

"How was the rest of the wedding? Is Dana upset?"

Gillian scoffs. "Why in the world would Dana be upset? You know her, she's –"

"Always thinking of everyone else," I finish.

"Exactly."

"How are you feeling?" I ask.

Stella wraps her arms around Gillian's waist. God, she's gotten so tall. "I got to feel the baby move!"

"And so did I," Axel says as he greets Orlie with a manly handshake.

"He cried. A lot." Stella grins.

"Yeah, I did. What's the problem with that, huh?" Axel shoots back.

The father and daughter sass each other back and forth, as is their way, and the rest of us laugh.

Soon after, Dana and Drew arrive with baby Mia. Mia is wide-eyed as she looks into the face of her baby cousin. *A baby? Like me? This won't do.* She descends into tears soon after and Drew comforts her in the corner while Dana takes a seat on the bed beside me to coo over Owen.

Harley and Amy arrive soon after. Harley is wearing a shit-eating grin.

"What is *that* smile about?"

"Nothing!" Amy answers on Harley's behalf. "Nothing at all."

"Sounds more like a threat than anything," Orlie remarks.

Amy glares at Harley. "You promised."

Harley glances at Grant and he shakes his head at her.

"What the heck is going on? Don't leave me out."

Amy stomps her feet. "I don't want to steal your spotlight."

I raise an eyebrow. "I mean, I'm the one who went into labor at Dana's wedding."

"Out of your control, Kiki," Dana reiterates.

I will feel guilty for that my whole life, no doubt.

"Tell us, Ames."

Amy looks up at Hunter. He shrugs. "If you want to, babe. Your call."

"Oh, my god," Gillian says. "Oh, my god, you're –"

"Don't say it before *she* can!" Harley snaps.

Gillian covers her mouth with her hand to keep from spoiling the surprise.

With a bashful smile, Amy announces, "I'm pregnant."

The whole room erupts with gasps and excitement.

"When will I get to rest?!" Dad cries out.

"Never, especially after the way you and Victoria went at each other on the dance floor," Harley says with a fake, playful glare.

Dad flushes and Grant glares at him. "Do you really have to bring that up? That's my sister you're talking about."

"What happened on the dance floor?" I cry out. "And Amy you're –"

I feel Orlie's hand on my back. "Take it easy, honey."

Owen starts to cry too, as if to make it doubly known I need to stay calm. "Okay, everyone, chill. I'm a mom now, so –"

The room settles as I rock Owen. He cries for a bit, but it's like music to my ears. I'm sure it won't be that way forever, but right now, this cry could be my favorite song.

Orlie protectively wraps an arm around me, softly caresses Owen's little head, the whisps of barely-there hair running through his fingers.

As my family settles around me, growing more and more engrossed in Owen settling into silence, I realize that for once I'm the center of attention and it's not freaking me out. This is how it is supposed to be. I don't need to be loud or wild or be anything but myself to stand out.

I've been enough for them all along. And I'm enough for Orlie too. He fell in love with me the way I am. Exactly the way I am. And he wouldn't change me. Wouldn't have me any other way.

I'm Kira Solace and that's enough.

"Oh, by the way," I say with a glimmering smile. "We're engaged."

The room erupts again, only for a moment before Owen stirs again. But everyone quiets down quickly enough for him to settle without much hassle.

"Congratulations, where is the ring?" Gillian asks.

Orlie hesitates. "It was a spur-of-the-moment thing."

"Oh, my god, boys!" Gillian snaps toward Axel, Grant, Hunter, and Drew. "You need to take him ring shopping ASAP."

"I'll schedule something with my people right now," Hunter says and whips out his phone.

I throw my head back in laughter. "No rush on the ring," I say to Orlie.

He looks down at my hand and shrugs. "You do look rather naked without one."

"I think I look rather naked without you kissing me right now," I say pointedly.

"Well, who am I to refuse that?"

As Orlie kisses me, the room erupts in the quietest of cheers in order not to disturb little Owen. I smile against my future husband's lips.

Life truly can change in the blink of an eye. I went from single girl to future single mother to girlfriend to now fiancé – and that might be an order that's kind of bungled.

However, I have a whole lifetime to look forward to with Orlie to do things in the right order...or however things decide to shake out. As long as I have my family on my team, the order of events doesn't matter.

We always land right in the love we've been searching for. Always.

30

———

KIRA

EPILOGUE

"Oh my gosh, he looks so nervous," Amy squeals as she peeks through the airy white curtain.

"Amy, stop that, you're just like the kids." Dana shoos our littlest sister away from the curtain. Although it's hard to see her as terribly little when she has her newborn daughter, Natalie, swaddled tight to her chest and little Jessica, who isn't so little anymore, leaning on her waist.

"How do you feel?" Harley asks me softly, touching my arm.

I shrug. "Fine."

She frowns. "Seriously."

"Um, yeah, I feel –" A fat baby hand covers my mouth softly. I look down into my son's eyes. Owen is now a little over a year old and, in that year, his eyes have transformed to be exactly like his father's. I rumble my lips against his hand and Owen laughs, removing his hand. "I feel fine."

Harley sighs. "You're awfully calm for your wedding day."

I laugh. Yes, it's my wedding day. But it's not extravagant like Amy's and Gillian's nor is it classic like Dana's and it's certainly not a courthouse wedding like Harley had.

It's simple. It's us.

Orlie and I decided that we wanted our wedding to be as easy and meaningful as possible for everyone. So, we're getting married in the backyard of my childhood home. Right now, we're posted up in the kitchen, waiting to go out there. The guest list is small, under seventy-five people, including only our closest friends and family.

We've opted to give a big fuck you to a lot of the classic wedding traditions. We're all wearing comfortable spring dresses. I let all my sisters pick out the one they liked best. That they felt most beautiful in. And I followed suit, wearing a delicate white dress that I'm sure will have dirty handprints all over it by the end of the night, courtesy of Owen.

For now, though, he's docile in my arms.

The most unconventional thing I wanted was for my sisters to walk down the aisle with their children. It felt wrong to exclude them. Would feel wrong to make my sisters stand in a line at the altar with me while their children squirmed in their seats, wishing they could sit with Mommy.

My dad only has two hands, after all.

"Okay, girls, positions please!" the wedding planner announces. "In reverse birth order, thanks!"

"Showtime!" Gillian grins, squeezing my arm. "See you out there."

I kiss my sister's cheek and then kiss baby Aurora who is babbling excitedly on Gillian's hip. Aurora came only a few months after Owen and is a carbon copy of her sister, Stella, when she was a baby, which reminds me –

"Good luck, Aunt Kira," Stella says, popping up beside me.

I can't believe how tall Stella has gotten over the past couple of years. Nearly ten years old, shooting up like a weed. "You look beautiful, Stell."

We hug as she takes her place next to Gillian, resting her head on her mother's arm.

"Thank god I don't have to carry a baby down the aisle, my lower back is killing me from these shoes," Harley groans, swooping little Tana by the hand and into their spot. Tana toddles excitedly, nearly tripping over her little fairy dress. Tana won't be an only child for long. When it became clear to Harley and Grant it would be harder to conceive another child than it was to conceive Tana, they immediately set their sights on adoption. They're heading to Haiti next month to collect their little boy, Henri.

From the corner, I hear a wail. "No!"

"Mia, you have to –" Dana coos gently, trying to pick Mia up off the ground.

"No, no, no! No up!" Dana and Drew's little one has gotten very good with her words, "no" being her favorite one.

"I have to pick you up for just a little bit, baby," she says.

"Walk," Mia says, crossing her chubby arms across her chest. She's also gotten very good at walking, a skill she apparently wants to show off today of all days.

Dana sighs.

"Dana," I call out, bobbing Owen on my knee. "It's fine. Let her walk."

"It will take forever, Kira," my older sister says.

"That's fine. We all get along just fine back here, don't we?" I twiddle my fingers against Owen's belly and he squeals with laughter.

I feel Dad's hand on my shoulder. "Kira's right. You take your time."

Smiling, I glance up at my dad. He's been rather quiet through all the hubbub of my sisters getting themselves and their little ones ready. In fact, he's been quiet for a while. Weeks if not months. Something's on his mind. I'm determined to find out what.

"Go," the wedding planner whispers to Amy.

While the wedding planner bids my sisters into their order, Dad and I hang back. Owen reaches his hands up to Dad. "You want Grandpa?"

"Yes, he does. Who doesn't want Grandpa?" Dad says, swiping Owen into his arms, peppering his chubby cheeks with kisses.

"Guess I should probably stand and act like I'm actually getting married," I say with a wry laugh. I get to my feet, spread my hands down my dress, and take a deep breath.

"You're remarkably calm. Never seen someone so calm," my dad says.

I shrug. "I don't know. Kind of just feels like another day. A great day, but still..." Just another step into my forever with Orlie. That's what it's like every day. Since Owen came into the world and our bond was sealed, Orlie and I have been a team. Strong and solid. Whether it's at the office working on our latest project or at home teaching our son 'The Itsy Bitsy Spider', we are a united front.

Dad wraps his arm around me and kisses the side of my head.

"Okay, last call –" Dana says from the doorway. "Am I picking her up or –"

"Let the girl walk, Dana!" Dad says.

The wedding planner holds the curtain open and Mia toddles through, Dana hurriedly grabbing her hand to help her down the step. "I'll give you two a moment," the planner says softly before scuttling outside.

Dad and I make our way to our spots and I take Owen back, tucking him onto my hip. His near-permanent spot. He's such a mommy's boy.

"How does it feel? Giving your last daughter away?"

"Uh –" He gives me a quick fleeting glance. "Good."

I narrow my eyes. "You okay?"

"Of course, I am," he says with a scoff. He pinches the curtain and looks through it. "Amy's right. He does look nervous."

"I wouldn't talk. That's going to be you soon."

Dad flushes deep crimson. "Don't say it so loud."

"No one is around!" I say with a laugh.

My father runs his hand through his grayish-blonde locks. "You sure you're comfortable with me proposing at your wedding?"

I grin. I couldn't think of a more perfect day for my father to propose to Victoria than the last Solace girl wedding. The two of them have been dating since the week after Dana and Drew's wedding. Amidst all the drama with my preterm labor, Dad was able to sweep under the rug that Victoria and him nearly kissed on the dance floor.

Sounds familiar.

A week later, Victoria abandoned a photoshoot in Buenos Aires to come all the way back to Burbank where she marched up to Dad's door and demanded, and this is, quote, "Either do something or stop looking at me with stars in your eyes."

Needless to say, he did something about it.

When he finally told us, no one was shocked, including Grant who had gone from disdaining his best friend dating his younger sister to quietly rooting for Dad to make a move.

Now, they've been together for a year and it's time Dad puts a ring on it.

"I won't make it a big thing," he says. "It'll be private, just me and her, but I don't want to steal any of your spotlight."

I rub my dad's arm. "Since when have I been concerned with anyone stealing my spotlight?"

I've come into my own the past two years, that much is true. No longer do I think I'm the quiet, mousey, forgettable Solace sister. But I haven't transformed into some social butterfly. I'm still me. I'm just more comfortable with it now.

I have Orlie to thank for that.

"Ma! Ma!"

And Owen.

My baby grabs me by the cheeks.

"You want a kiss, don't you?" I give him several smooches and he is sated, resting his head on my shoulder, his dark baby hair skimming my skin. "God, why don't they stay this small?"

Dad wraps his arms around me and Owen, nuzzling my hair softly. "Now you understand why I've been a wreck the past four years."

We remain there for a long moment until the wedding planner pops his head in and whispers. "Ready?"

"Ready as I'll –" I start, taking a step forward.

Dad jerks me back. "Wait a second –"

I look back at him; there's something in his eyes. That's tremoring, fighting to be spoken. I glance at the wedding planner. "Just another minute?"

He does his best not to roll his eyes. "I'll try and stave off any whispers of a runaway bride."

I laugh. "Thank you." If anyone would think for a second I'd run away from today, they don't know me at all.

"Dad, what's going on?"

He takes a deep breath. "I have something that's been on my mind and I wanted to wait to tell you girls until after your wedding, but I can't keep it in and you're the only one I know who can keep a secret so –"

I furrow my brow. "Is something wrong?"

"Wrong?! No, not wrong, not..." He smiles. Eyes glistening. "You know I love you girls more than anything, right?"

I smile, feeling a swell of emotions. Kent Solace is super dad. When Mom left, who stepped up to do the work of two parents instead of just one? He did. Who is the most loving and supportive father a girl could ask for? He is. Who deserves happiness more than everyone after putting the happiness of his daughters ahead of his at every turn? He does.

"You can't make me cry before I even get down the aisle, Daddy."

"I'm sorry, I'm..." He pinches the bridge of his nose. "I don't want you to ever feel like I'm choosing someone else over you."

"By being with Victoria? Daddy, we all love Vic."

"I know, but –"

"You've been on your own for so long...all any of us have wanted is for you to find love like we all have." I glance at Owen who is now sleeping on my shoulder. Loving Orlie was one gift, but loving my child with him has been that times one million.

Dad runs his hand through Owen's silky hair and then looks at me. "Kira. Victoria and I are going to have a baby."

My heart leaps into my throat. "You mean eventually or like..."

He shakes his head. "Like it's already happening."

I'm speechless. Words cannot begin to encapsulate the overwhelming happiness I feel.

"We were trying, I'm not as careless as you girls. Just since I'm...getting old and I don't want to be totally senile by the time they graduate high school but –"

"Oh, Daddy..." Tears start to run down my face.

He chews his lower lip. "Are you upset? I know it's weird thinking about your old dad having –'"

"No, Daddy, no..." I throw my arm around him and squeeze him tight.

No wonder he's been acting weird the past couple of weeks. "I'm so happy for you."

Nothing could be better than my dad finding love and getting a second go at the life he thought he had the first time. I know he doesn't regret his relationship with our mother for a single second. After all, he has five girls who are all kicking ass and taking names.

But he deserves a happily ever after too.

"Psst."

I glare at the wedding planner who is once again peeping through the curtain.

"The string quartet is getting restless. You're on."

I start to protest, but my father takes a step forward and holds out his arm. "Come on, Kira. Time to get married."

Tentatively, I take a step forward, sliding my arm through my father's, hoisting Owen higher on my hip. "I think I just got nervous."

"Don't be," Dad says with a smile.

Through the curtain, we hear the beginnings of the wedding march. The wedding planner pulls the curtain aside, revealing the backyard, the aisle created from rose petals. And at the end of the aisle is Orlie.

He looks incredible. Usually, he's much more at home in a three-piece suit, but the dressed-down khaki sport coat suits him.

I immediately see the breath freeze in his chest. Trevor reaches out and touches Orlie's shoulder. We chose Trevor as our officiant, considering how much of a part he played in bringing us together.

Now, here we are. Face to face, our fathers at our sides. And we're about to be married.

The butterflies in my belly start batting their wings.

"Let's do this, huh?" Dad says.

I smile at him. "Yeah. Let's do it."

We walk down the aisle, step by step. The closer we come to the head of the aisle, the redder Orlie's eyes become until a few tears tumble down his cheeks.

Dad and I come to a stop. And I feel a little faint. This is it. The end of the unmarried Solace sisters. Of course, it's just a symbol. We're all still close as ever, seeing each other as often as possible. But I can't help but think this is the end of an era.

"I love you," Dad whispers and kisses my cheek. He touches Owen's back, smiling. I get an image of him with his own little one someday very soon. I can't wait to see my dad become one all over again. "Orlie –" He reaches his hand out to Orlie and pulls him into a hug. "Be good to her."

"Always."

Trevor also snags a hug before Dad goes to take his seat. Though I'm completely caught up in Orlie and this moment, I have to watch as he settles in beside Victoria. The look of love in their eyes is more potent than ever as she reaches for his arm as he sits. Unable to resist touching him.

Wanting him as close as possible as their love manifests in a totally new way inside her.

"Can I?" Orlie says, gesturing to Owen.

"Oh, yeah, please, my arms are killing me," I say.

Everyone laughs.

Orlie slides Owen out of my arms, whispering in my ear in that brief moment of contact, "You look beautiful."

I adjust my glasses and flush. Has the same ring as the very first time he ever said it.

Owen does not wake up fully, simply adjusting his hand to grab onto the lapel of Orlie's jacket.

"You kids ready?" Trevor asks.

Orlie and I exchange smiles. "I think so," I say.

With a clearing of his throat, Trevor begins the ceremony. It is lighthearted and earnest as he tells the tale of Orlie and Kira and the love that they both resisted for so long. Though we've asked him to keep the ceremony short (for the children's sake), he can't help but wax poetic. At least he knows how to hold the attention of the crowd.

"Orlie and Kira have written their own vows for the occasion," Trevor says. "Orlie, you're up."

Orlie flushes as he hands Owen over to Trevor. He reaches out and takes my hands. "Kira. I believed for a long time I had a hardened heart. Or no heart at all. Turns out, I was just keeping it buried deep inside. And then you came along and you reached in and grabbed it, no holds barred."

I hear my sisters laugh. *Classic Kira.*

"I couldn't help falling in love with you. You're the smartest woman I know. The best mother to our son."

My heart leaps as I glance at Owen who is quietly tugging on a lock of Trevor's long white hair.

"And all I want for the rest of my life is to love and be loved by you."

I can practically hear all our guests swoon. "You memorized all of that, huh?"

They laugh as Orlie blushes hard. "I practiced a lot."

"It was perfect," I say with a giggle, tipping forward onto the balls of my feet. All I want is to kiss him right now. But we still have a bit to go before that.

"I guess, it's my turn."

I start to reach into my pocket for the vows I'd written out, perfected over the past couple of months. But then I stop. I look out at the first row where my sisters sit with their husbands and their children. They're all smiling at me.

"I got quite an education in love before I fell in love with you, Orlie." I take his hands tighter. "Each of my sisters taught me a really important lesson. From Harley I learned to throw caution to the wind –"

I see Grant and Harley exchange a look and laugh, Tana looking up at them with confusion.

I then look to Gillian and Axel. Aurora is balanced on Axel's knee while Stella is leaning into Gillian's lap.

"Gillian taught me that the best of things take time. And Amy, she showed me that the best of things can happen when you least expect them." I grin at Hunter and Amy and their two girls, Jessica and Natalie. "In the most unlikely of places, too."

My attention snaps to Dana who has already started crying, close to weeping, trying to wipe away her tears with tissue after tissue from the box in her lap. "Dana taught me patience. And how to give with your whole heart while asking for nothing in return."

Drew rubs my sister's knee, his other arm wrapped around Mia.

"Even if you deserve the whole world," I add. "Just like Dana does."

"Oh my god, I can't do this," Dana says, waving her hands in front of her face.

"And then there's my dad."

Dad straightens up in his seat. Victoria looks up at him with the utmost love in her eyes. I never thought I'd see someone look at my dad like that again.

"Daddy, you showed me what a real man looks like. Someone who is kindhearted isn't afraid to be vulnerable with those he loves, and lets himself change in order to be the best man he can be for those he loves."

My dad's eyebrows rise, lips tightening, clearly holding back tears. Victoria rubs his arm and whispers something in his ear.

I return my gaze to Orlie. "Still, with all of those lessons, I managed to bungle the first part of our relationship."

Everyone laughs, including Orlie. "Not just you, Kira," he says.

"But I promise for the rest of our lives to give my best self to you. Because I see you give your best self to me. And to Owen. Everyday. And I hope I give even a pinch of what you give."

"You do," Orlie whispers. "You do, baby."

I shake my head. "I want to grow with you. I want t-to do life with you. With all its twists and turns. You make me feel capable and powerful and seen in ways I've never felt."

I pull his hands to my sternum, closing the space between us. "So, I think I'll marry you if that's alright."

More laughter. Orlie smiles. "More than alright with me."

With the vows done, we exchange our rings, and then, the moment I've waited for since the moment I saw him at the end of the aisle.

"Excuse me for the tears –" Trevor says weepily. "I've

felt like Kira's been one of my own for years now. And now she really is, so by the power vested in me –"

Owen's head pops up and he reaches for me. "Ma!"

I scoop him into my arms from Trevor and nuzzle his cheek. "Owen!"

"By the state of California, I now pronounce you husband and wife! Orlie, you may kiss the bride."

Orlie embraces me, Owen between us, looking sleepy and confused. He touches my cheek and kisses me with all his gentleness. "I love you."

I kiss him again, harder. There'll be more of that tonight, that's for sure. "I love you."

"And you too, baby boy," Orlie says, kissing Owen's forehead.

"Introducing Mr. and Mrs. –"

"I'm keeping my last name, Trevor!" I call out.

"Listen, it doesn't have the same ring to say Mr. Wynters and Ms. Solace!"

Orlie and I laugh as the string quartet begins the recessional music. He slings his arm around my shoulder. "I think you taught us all a lesson too, Kira."

"Oh? What's that?"

With a sentimental look at my family, he beams. "Be grateful for where you come from."

These words ring in my brain the rest of the night as we embrace, laugh, and dance. We've had a lot of heartbreak in our lives, us girls. But without it, we never would have found our way here. Totally in love with our lives, our husbands, our children.

And with love *that* powerful, there's no telling what kind of heights our happiness will reach.

www.ingramcontent.com/pod-product-compliance
Lightning Source LLC
Chambersburg PA
CBHW021346150726
47989CB00005B/2126